KARZIN

CONQUERED WORLD: BOOK SEVEN

ELIN WYN

ANNIE

I used to be a heavy sleeper. A bomb could go off and I wouldn't stir.

Then one day, a bomb did go off.

Now, the slightest noise brought me out of my slumber.

This morning, it was the soft sigh of my younger sister, Cassie, as she rolled over on her sleeping mat.

Usually, it was my older brother Helix that woke me. He often talked in his sleep. He used to be a city official in Duvest before the sky cracked open and everything changed.

Once I was awake, there was no going back to sleep. I squinted across the room to the clock placed on the floor and sighed. I would've had to get up soon anyway.

At least now I could take a little extra time with breakfast.

It was hard to move quietly in the house. It consisted of only two rooms, not including a washroom, and was built almost entirely of scrap. From the outside, our house looked like pieces of four different houses stitched together. One of our walls was entirely metal and slightly curved. Apparently, it came from the alien space ship that had defeated the Xathi.

Helix refused to touch that wall. His sleeping mat was placed as far away from it as it possibly could be. He didn't have anything against the aliens that had saved our planet.

He'd be a fool if he did. But he didn't like anything that reminded him of the Xathi.

Helix was on duty when the Xathi swarmed Duvest. He faced one head-on in order to give people a chance to escape. He survived, but only just. The Xathi took off the lower half of his left leg. Helix was retired from being a city official with the highest honors, but that hadn't helped him find work since.

The floor creaked under my feet. It wasn't a proper floor, just rows of flat-ish planks lined up next to each other to keeps us off the dirt. I heard my father snore in the other room. He and my mother used to own a general goods store. The Xathi destroyed that, too.

"Andromeda, be quiet," Cassie groaned. "I only got home an hour ago."

Andromeda was my full first name. I had no idea what possessed my mother to give me such a formal, old-fashioned name. For as long as I remembered, I'd insisted on going by Annie.

Cassie only called me Andromeda when she was in a foul mood, which was more often than not.

"That's not my fault, Cassiopeia," I snapped, invoking her equally awful first name in return. "What are you even doing out so late at night?"

"Pretending I live anywhere but here," she replied.

"If you got a job, you could live somewhere else," I replied.

"I guess I won't be sleeping in this morning," Helix groaned.

"Sorry, Helix," Cassie mumbled. She didn't mind vexing me, but she hated disrupting Helix.

"Any plans today?" I asked him.

"Liddy Burris is trying to open up a grocery on the other end of town. I'm going to offer to do her books," he replied.

"I think that would suit you," I smiled.

"Me, too," Cassie grinned. "Want some coffee?"

"I'm the oldest. Neither of you should be babying me," Helix chuckled.

"We don't baby you," Cassie said defensively.

Maybe we did baby him. A little.

"Cass, do you even know how to use the coffee maker?" Helix asked.

"Annie does." Cassie jerked her chin in my direction. I bought the coffee maker last week. The week before, I bought a hot plate and skillet. Both were placed on the floor in the corner farthest from our sleeping mats.

Next week, I wanted to buy a bigger food storage unit. The one we had now didn't keep perishables well enough. We couldn't afford to keep throwing away food. Rent was due next week, as well. It wasn't much. Everyone living in Somerst paid a monthly fee to keep the town running. I paid my own, as well as the fees for the rest of my family.

I opened the storage unit and pulled out three eggs. A quick sniff told me they were still edible but I would have to go to the market today after work. The cheese had gone bad overnight. That's what you got when you bought stuff that they were ready to throw out because it was the only thing you could afford.

I opened a window and tossed the cheese out onto the unpaved road. Somerst had yet to develop a suitable waste disposal system. The City of Nyheim offered to collect our waste for a fee, but everyone in Somerst agreed the fee was too high.

Councilwoman Vidia assured us she was working on a solution.

"Cheese is bad. But the bread is still good." I held up a bagged loaf of dark brown bread.

"I wouldn't call that bread good," Helix joked.

"It won't poison you," I corrected with a laugh. I'd met others who'd suffered injuries at the hands of the Xathi. Many were angry, many were sad. Helix always had a smile on his face. His sense of humor never faltered. He was my hero for that.

"That's all a man can ask for nowadays," he replied.

"Is there any butter?" Cassie asked.

"We finished it two days ago," I reminded her. "I'll pick more up tonight."

"Eggs and dry toast for breakfast then?" she grumbled. I ignored her as I cracked the eggs into the skillet and turned on the hot plate.

"I hope Liddy Burris does manage that grocery. The market in Nyheim is always so crowded."

"Go at a less busy time, then," Cassie suggested.

"I would, except I work, like so many others do," I sighed. "Why can't you get a job, again?"

"Nowhere will take me," Cass replied. "I've asked everyone in this heap of wreckage."

"This heap of wreckage is your home, Cass." Helix had a warning tone in his voice. It was slight, but it was enough to get Cassie to change her tone.

"Not for long," she said. "We'll all move to a nice big house again. We'll all have our own rooms again."

"How about you ride into Nyheim with me? There's plenty of jobs there," I suggested. Cassie opened her mouth to speak. No doubt she had an excuse prepared in advanced, but Helix gave her a look.

"That's a good idea," Cass said.

She was in her first year of university when the Xathi attacked. The college still hadn't reopened.

"Maybe there's an opening at my lab," I said brightly.

"No offense, but you have the dullest job on the planet," Cass replied.

"The job isn't dull. My assignments are dull." I was a geologist in Nyheim. I had the least seniority out of all the other workers, so I always got the short end of the stick when it came to jobs. I didn't mind, though. I still got a decent paycheck.

"Still going to have to pass," Cass replied. "You're burning the eggs."

"I am not. I don't like runny eggs." I scrambled the eggs with a wooden spoon, except the spoon part broke off a few weeks ago.

"Take some off for me then." Cass grabbed one of our chipped plates. "I need something to soften the toast." I scrapped some gooey eggs onto her plate and placed a piece of bread on the part of the hotplate not covered by the skillet. Cass grabbed the bread before it was toasty and devoured everything on her plate in less than a minute.

"I'm going to wash up. I shouldn't smell like I slept on the floor when I apply for jobs," she declared.

"Don't use all the hot water," I warned her. After Cassie shut the door, I turned to Helix. "She's going to melt my brain."

"Remember, she's only known the cushy life. She didn't have to help mom and dad in the shop like we did," Helix said. Our parents' shop really took off when Cassie was five and too young to be useful. Helix and I spent most of our childhood sweeping, counting, and stocking. For most of Cassie's life, she'd wanted for nothing.

"She doesn't wear hardship well." I grabbed another plate and scooped a generous portion of eggs for Helix.

"Put some of mine back. There's not enough for you," he insisted.

"There's plenty for me," I replied. "Besides, I can always pick up something else in the city."

"You shouldn't have to," Helix said. "You do everything for us. The least we can do is give you the lion's share of breakfast."

"That would be silly, considering you're the lion of the family," I smiled.

"I still have no idea what a lion looks like," Helix laughed. That was one of the many inside jokes we shared as a family. Dad thought it was funny to use Earth expressions that made little sense here on

Ankou. Don't wake the bear was a particular favorite of his.

"I think it has green scales and twenty eyes," I said.

"No way. A lion breathes fire and has three legs," he insisted.

"You win. Breathing fire is way cooler than twenty eyes," I admitted. Steam pouring from underneath the bathroom door caught my eye. I groaned and stood from my crouched position over the skillet.

"Cass, easy on the hot water!" I banged on the door.

"You're going to bring the walls down if you keep banging like that!" my mother called from the other room. I rolled my eyes and said nothing. I was well into my twenties, but that didn't stop my mother from scolding me like a toddler.

"I'm going to fetch more water," I told Helix. "Cass is bound to use it all. Can you watch my food?"

"You got it," Helix grinned.

I opened our flimsy front door and grabbed the bucket sitting just outside. Lucky for us, we lived close to the water dispensary. The line was long, but it moved quickly. We were only allowed to fill up one bucket at a time to make sure the well didn't run dry.

When I brought the filled bucket back to the house, I dumped its contents into our water tank. Just as I thought, Cassie nearly used up all of it. Dad would need to get more.

When I went back into the house, Cassie was still in the shower. She must've planned this. She knew I wouldn't risk being late to work.

"Crap," I groaned. "I have to go."

"What about breakfast?" Helix asked.

"Just eat my eggs. I don't have time," I urged him. "Tell Cassie her plan worked."

KARZIN

"Pardon me, leader Karzin. You have guests."

I turned to see Pem, one of the Urai, standing behind me at the command center doors of the *Aurora,* his arms clasped behind his back.

"What do you mean, that I have guests? Who?" This was not something I wanted, nor had the patience for.

Pem, with a passive look of indifference, touched his speech pad with his left hand. "They are members of your strike team. They have come to speak with you."

With a nod, he turned and fairly floated out of the command center. Despite living with them, I was still bewildered by the way they moved, so smoothly, effortlessly, and fluidly.

With a string of curses that had become part of my regular vocabulary, I left the command center and headed to meet the team. I crossed over the open-air bridge back into the middle section of the ship and passed by a mirror.

I stopped. My long hair was gone, I had chopped most of it off months ago. Now, it was a disheveled clump that reminded me of a bird's nest. My once clean-shaven face was filled with three days of stubble, and even my purple shoulder bands seemed to be losing their luster. I stormed away from the mirror, if the men couldn't deal with how I looked, then it didn't matter to me.

They were waiting for me in what had become the common area when anyone returned to the *Aurora*.

Iq'her, with his bright green circuitry shining along his bald scalp down along his arms, sat in one of the chairs, playing with his knife.

Sylor, the one that would be my second, my cousin, at least in species, leaned against a wall, his green skin matching the large plant he was studying.

Then, the brothers. Rokul and his silent brashness, Takar and his attempt to show himself as a sophisticated, well-educated man, both standing in the center of the room, watching the hall which I entered from. Their matching reddish-orange skin shone in the light, their scalps still shaved everywhere but in the middle, where they both insisted on spiking it from front to back.

"What is it? I'm busy," I said as I entered the common area and leaned on a table. Unless this was a mission, I had no interest in what they had to say.

"Ah, the 'I'm busy' claim that you have been so apt to use these months," Takar scoffed.

I looked at him for a single moment, then turned my attention to Sylor. "Why are you here? Is there something that needs to be done?"

The look he gave me showed concern, and anger. "We need to talk, about you."

Of course. "What is there to talk about? I'm doing my job while the four of you are off doing whatever it is that humans do."

Sylor left his position by the plant and approached me. His left hand, forever mangled in a long-ago attack by the Xathi, twitched slightly. "That's the problem. You look at us as though we have forgotten who and what we are."

"Haven't you?" I was loud and didn't care. They, and the others, had forgotten where we come from, and what happened to us, to our peoples, to our families. "Haven't you forgotten what's happened and is still happening? But, instead of looking for a way to get off the planet and return home, you've decided to 'settle' here and forget everything."

"We haven't forgotten. Nothing can make us forget," Takar started.

I wasn't going to let him lie to me. "Don't give me that!" I yelled. "Don't you *dare* tell me that you haven't forgotten. You, your brother, the rest of the entire crew have given up!" A bit of spittle flew from my mouth as I spoke, so I wiped my mouth.

I could see the anger growing in Takar.

"You dare accuse us of forgetting and giving up? We," he pointed between his brother and himself, "lost family to the Xathi, as well. And," he said, his voice calming and growing quiet, "unlike you, we know that our family is dead. We watched them die before our eyes. The idea that there are still Xathi *anywhere* in the universe boils my blood and angers me, but I have also come to learn that, at the moment, there is nothing that can be done by our hands. My brother and I have not forgotten, we have merely moved on, for now."

I looked between them all. Rokul nodded, Iq'her looked more interested in his knife, and Sylor crossed his arms as he looked at me. "What you're trying to say to me, is that you're…what…waiting for the right moment to find a way back home?"

Rokul shook his head and took a seat. Sylor simply stared at me, and Takar walked away, leaving the room.

It was Iq'her, in his formal tones, that answered my question. "What they are trying to say, sir, is that we are trying to make the best of the situation that is at hand. You, of all people, sir, should understand that there are times when you must step back in order to better fortify a position or to better assess a situation."

"Oh, so this is a strategic thing? Is that it?" I knew they were trying to move me, to…how did the humans say it…con me. They were saying what they thought needed to be said in order to sway me.

With a movement quicker than I could follow, Iq'her put his knife away and shot to his feet. He was in front of me, in my face, rage in his eyes. "I have followed you, I have listened to you, I have respected you like no other person in my life. It was you that saved me from my own darkness, and you speak to me in this way. You are no longer the man, no longer the leader, that I knew. You are a fool."

I shoved him away from me as hard as I could. "I'm the fool? Me?! I'm the only one that's still looking for a way home! I'm the only one that still cares!"

That might have been over the line. The pain in Iq'her's eyes was mirrored on Rokul's face. Sylor stared at the ceiling, his shoulders sagging. I didn't care. "I'm the only one…"

"Still trying?" Sylor finished for me. "You were about to say that, correct? You're the one that has given up." He walked towards me, put his hand on Iq'her's shoulder and gently pulled him away.

When Iq'her went back to his seat, Sylor took his place in front of me. "You've locked yourself away here, for weeks, months on end. You refuse to leave, you refuse to acknowledge that, at least for now, Ankou is our home, and refuse to accept the fact that when we left our homes, the Xathi were unstoppable."

"There is a chance that our homes have been destroyed and nothing is left of them," Takar said as he came back into the room. "The Xathi were…relentless and savage in their attacks. I know that there was nothing left of our own world when they were finished."

I knew that Takar and Rokul were from one of the secondary systems in Skotan space. Few of those planets had survived the initial Xathi attack.

Sylor, with a short nod, turned back to me. "Their attack upon Valorn was devastating. We were already losing, badly. There is a chance that the fight there has already been lost."

I had had enough. I was finished with them.

"Then you have forgotten how strong our people really are. *True* Valorni do not give up the battle, and I refuse to forget our people, our families, or what our responsibility is. If you have nothing else for me except useless comments about my actions or my behavior, then I suggest you leave, now," I growled.

"No. We're here to fix whatever this is and get the real Karzin back," Rokul said from his chair. "We need you back, sir."

I shook my head, waved them off, and left the common area. "You know how to leave," I called back behind me. I returned to the command center and finished working on the defective computer core. I needed to get it back into space, back to the satellite it had come from, and back to work on finding a signal.

While I worked, I watched them leave through one of the outer surveillance cameras. They opened a rift and walked through, the rift closing behind them.

It was about time they left, they had wasted enough of my time.

If they couldn't understand what I was doing, I wanted nothing to do with them. I needed to put my concentration into this.

"Leader Karzin?" It was Pem,again. I turned to look at him. "Might I ask you a question?"

"Fine. What is it?"

He walked closer to me, his left hand on his speech-box. "Your men seem to be...very passionate about your current state of affairs."

"What of it?"

"I was curious as to why you and your men have such a differing set of opinions. Do you not believe in your cause upon this world?"

"Our *cause*, as you put it, is over. The Xathi have been destroyed here and the humans are safe. It's time we return home, to *our* home. That is my cause now."

"And if there is no way to return to your home?" he asked.

I never answered him.

Because it simply wasn't an option.

I couldn't let it be.

ANNIE

Thanks to Cassie's little stunt, I was running late. I didn't get to shower before work. I barely got to run a comb through my hair and brush my teeth. My nice pants were wrinkled after hanging on the line to dry. My stomach growled in protest to skipping breakfast and my minimalist dinner the night before.

I jumped on the shuttle seconds before the doors closed. There were no seats, but that was normal. I grabbed on to the first solid, non-living thing I felt just as the shuttle took off. Most of the seats were filled by people just like me, harried and trying to get to work.

A few of the passengers were of alien species. The first time I saw one riding the shuttle, I couldn't stop staring. I felt so rude, but I couldn't help it. I'd never been that close to an alien before. Now, though I was still curious about them, I was more used to the sight.

There were three separate species of aliens that now lived alongside us. There were the Skotan, red from head to toe with some kind of retractable scales, though I'd never seen them in person. K'ver were gray and appeared to have circuits embedded directly into their skin. Two of them had taken jobs at my lab in the tech innovations department. I smiled to them in passing but I'd yet to have a chance to speak to one. The Valorni were green and built like barns. I saw them the least out of all the species. Their natural strength made them ideal for labor-oriented jobs. It was likely that a Valorni built the house I lived in now.

Some still treated the aliens with skepticism, but I saw no reason to. If they wanted to do us harm, they wouldn't have risked so much to save our world from the Xathi. I'd heard they couldn't leave the planet now. They'd trapped themselves here to save us.

That earned each one of them respect in my book.

The shuttle ride was brief, but I still had a distance to walk until I reached my office.

Nyheim used to be spectacular. In a way, it still was, but it was a beauty of the spirit, not the eye. It had survived so much and still stood strong. Most of its memorable structures were gone now.

Bare bones of buildings in disrepair lined the

streets. It was more like walking through a skeleton of a city than an actual city.

Halfway between the shuttle station and my office was a tiny eatery made out of a dislodged shipping container. Orlin, the owner, furnished the inside with a small kitchen and cut windows in the sides to take orders.

"How's it going, Annie?" he asked when I stepped up to the window. "Cassie make you late again?"

"You know it," I sighed. Because of Cassie, I was forced to grab breakfast from Orlin at least once a week. I didn't mind, though. Orlin was a fantastic cook. He could make even meal rations taste high class.

"Have you told her I'm hiring?" he asked. "I'm getting too old to be working here every day."

"You're not getting old," I said with a dismissive wave. Orlin was barely fifty and in great shape for his age. Though I could understand wanting a day off every now and then. I was going on my twelfth day straight. "I almost got her on the shuttle today. If I told her I wanted her to work here, she'd never come. I have to trick her somehow."

"Good luck with that," Orlin chuckled. "Your usual, then?"

"Please." I reached into my back to pull out my credit chip, but Orlin waved me off.

"You've got enough to worry about. I'm not going to

make you worry about food on top of it all," he said.

"Thanks, Orlin," I grinned. I stood off to the side while Orlin made a fresh pot of coffee and flakey croissant with egg, cheese, butter, *and* a small piece bacon. If Cassie knew, I bet she'd change her tune about coming to the city with me. We never had enough to afford bacon on top of our regular groceries. Meat had become a rarity since most of the domesticated animals were killed or escaped during the Xathi invasion and many of the wild creatures moved to other areas.

Orlin handed me my coffee and food. I flashed him another grateful smile before continuing on my way. The croissant was devoured by the time I reached my building.

The top half of my office building was gone. A tarp was stretched over the gap to make a ceiling, but no one used that floor anyway. My lab was on the third floor, untouched by the Xathi ship during its initial crash landing.

I was lucky to have this job. My last place of employment closed down not long after the Xathi ship crashed onto our planet. I applied to my current job, expecting nothing, but I was pleasantly surprised. All of the sciences were in demand as everyone scrambled to get back to pre-war levels of industry.

I'd barely stepped into the room when one of my colleagues ran up to me. Bea was a woman in her mid-thirties who always wore her black hair in a bun so tight I couldn't imagine how it wasn't painful for her. She had yet to speak to me at all since I started working here. Honestly, no one here had been very social, so if Bea was running up to me, either something terrible or something fantastic had happened.

"You've got to see this!" she exclaimed. "I've never seen anything like it."

"What?" I asked. Bea grabbed my arm and tugged me through the lobby of the building.

"I came into the main labs, yeah? And all I could hear were these piercing beeps and alarms," she spoke quickly.

"A malfunction, then?" I asked.

"That's what I thought! Especially once I realized they were coming from your station, no offense," she looked over her shoulder and shot me a look of apology.

"My station?" I stammered. I could understand her surprise. My station was always silent.

I'd been assigned a task that initially sounded interesting. My job was to monitor the area around the remains of the half of the Xathi ship that had crashed back down to the planet's surface. I traveled out to the wreckage myself and placed all sorts of scanners and monitors on the surface of the earth and beneath it at various intervals.

The main concern was unknown substances leaking from the Xathi ship and negatively affecting the soil around it. Though, since the Xathi ship's remains were far out in the desert, where no humans had ever settled, there wasn't much of a risk factor. It was mainly for scientific curiosity.

I thought it was going to be such an exciting job. I thought I'd be at the forefront of discoveries, unveiling the mysteries of the giant crystal insects that attacked us. However, it had been nearly two months and nothing had happened yet.

Until now, apparently.

"I'm sure it was just a glitch," I said lamely.

"I checked!" Bea cried. "I assumed it was a glitch, too. Again, no offense."

"None taken," I muttered.

"There's nothing wrong with any of your consoles. All of your monitors are in working order but they're recording stuff that's off the charts. Literally!" Bea dragged me into the elevator and pushed the button for our floor at least twenty times before the doors closed.

"How many caffeine pills have you had today, Bea?" I asked. I once saw a whole bottle of caffeine tablets at her station. It wasn't uncommon for everyone, other than me, to work late into the night on their various assignments.

"I've been here for nearly twenty-four hours," Bea said.

"What? That's not healthy!" I exclaimed.

"I have so much to finish up! Didn't I tell you? I'm transferring at the end of the week," she replied. I wanted to tell her that since she'd never spoken to me before now that of course she didn't tell me she was transferring, but I refrained.

"You're transferring?" I asked.

"My husband got a job in Kaster. It pays too well for us to say no," she explained. If she kept talking as fast as she was, she was going to bite her tongue clean off.

"Is there much work for a botanist in Kaster?" I asked, praying that she actually was a botanist.

"There's lots of work for botanists everywhere nowadays," she replied.

I tried not to audibly sigh with relief. "The Xathi did a number on the local plant life. There's so much to study, I'll have my hands full for months. Bet you wish you'd studied botany now, don't you?" She nudged me playfully and cackled a little too loudly.

"Promise me you won't take any more of those pills, okay?" I patted her shoulder.

"Don't worry, I've emptied the bottle."

"That makes me more worried," I winced.

The world's slowest elevator finally arrived at our floor. Bea dragged me out of the elevator and through the double doors of the main lab. I heard the beeping alarms before we entered the room. I half expected the alarms to be nothing more than a side effect of Bea's excessive caffeine intake.

"See? It's going at it again!" she exclaimed.

"Please sit down," I urged. "I'm worried you're going to have a heart attack."

My station was in the farthest corner of the room. All of the monitors I'd placed out in the desert corresponded to a light on my console. All of them were flashing green, a sign of change in the environment.

"What could this be?" I muttered to myself as I approached the console. The first thing I noticed was that all of the monitors were no longer where I'd placed them. They'd been shifted considerably. Some looked like they were buried far deeper than I'd left them. That could've only happened if the earth itself had shifted.

I pulled up a seismograph that reflected any changes in the amount of energy coursing through the planet's crust. The graph showed that huge spikes of energy had been bursting from the earth all night.

"So, what's happening?" Bea appeared at my side, startling me.

"I don't know," I replied. "But something out there is causing tremors bigger than anything I've ever seen."

KARZIN

It didn't come as a surprise that, not long after the team's failed attempt to intervene upon my behavior, I received a summons from General Rouhr.

While I had never imagined that any of our crew would ever forsake our homes, the idea that General Rouhr had abandoned his own home in favor of this human planet surprised me more than anything else.

The man that had faced down Xathi hordes, fought them to within a breath of death, and vowed to not let the Xathi destroy this world or its inhabitants.

But he had abandoned his own world because he had found a human woman that changed him.

I had no desire to go to Nyheim. Even with a rift, it would be a waste of my time. However, it was my duty to go.

I cleaned myself up, had one of the Urai cut my hair to ensure it was as it should be, and I shaved. While I had come to like the beard I had begun to grow, it was unprofessional. With a clean uniform, I asked Fen to open a rift for me to Nyheim and I passed through.

I had been through several rifts, yet the shuddering cold never became easier. Fen had set the rift for just outside the city to ensure that no one accidentally passed through it, and I was grateful. The fifteen-minute walk to General Rouhr's new offices would give me an opportunity to gain control of myself. I did not wish to show my disdain for his actions, and I needed the time to hide it.

The building that he used for his offices also contained the offices for his human mate, Vidia. She had taken over as some sort of leader for the human population and had convinced Rouhr to join her. While still our commander, he was now a liaison of sorts between our peoples.

It was a step down from what he should be.

I entered the building and was greeted by an overly excitable—or peppy, as the humans would say—young human male with a very light voice. "Commander Karzin. It's such a pleasure to see you. How are you?" His smile made me want to punch him, repeatedly.

"My well-being is not of your concern. I am here for General Rouhr."

With an over-exaggerated wave of his arms, he seemed to just let my comment roll off. "Of course you are. He's right this way. I'll take you to him." His enthusiasm grated on my nerves. I knew where the general's office was, I didn't need an escort.

"I know the way," I told him.

As if he hadn't heard my statement, he continued on with his rambling monologue. "He's such a wonderful man, the general is. He's done such wonderful things while working here. And the work he's done with Ms. Vidia, oh my, I just can't believe how amazing and wonderful they are for us. Here you go, Commander."

He stood at the general's door, his hand on the knob, waiting for me to come close. He opened it for me and smiled as I walked in.

Before I could say anything, he called out loudly from behind me, "Commander Karzin for you, General."

"Thank you, Tobias. That will be all." The general was sitting at his desk, and I had to admit that he did look less haggard than he had months ago when we were still fighting the Xathi. He looked years younger and much healthier.

I stood at attention, giving the general a salute. "I am here as requested, sir."

Of course.

My team sat in the office, watching me.

"You don't look happy about it." I looked at the general, my anger seething inside of me. "As a matter of fact," he continued, "you look even more pissed than normal."

"I'm sorry, sir. I don't know what you mean," I responded.

"My apologies. I've begun to pick up on the human vernacular and I seem to be using more and more. You look angry." He folded his hands on the desk and leaned forward a little. "Are you angry at being called here?"

I took a deep breath to gather myself before answering. "No, sir. Merely curious. How can I be of service?"

"So, you're not upset at seeing your team here the day after their failed attempt at an intervention to get you out of the *Aurora*?" the general asked, a hint of a smile on his face.

I didn't answer.

The fact that even asked the question meant he already knew the answer. My team had come to complain to the general like petulant children.

"I see," he nodded. "You think they've come crying to father. It's sad that you think that, because that's not at all what you're here for," the general said as he took to his feet. "I actually have a job for you and your team."

"My apologies then, sir. What is the mission?" I

knew I should have felt a bit of shame for my attitude, but I didn't.

He pointed behind me. "May I introduce Dr. Annie Parker?"

I turned to see a human woman, someone I had not noticed when I first came in. A shock of warmth ran through me. An appreciation of a form, nothing more, surely.

I did not wish to lust after human women. But if I did...this would be the woman to do it for.

She was small enough that, when seated, she'd been hidden behind the brothers. When she stood, I saw a small woman, no more than five feet tall, with painfully straight red hair that stood out brightly against her pale, alabaster skin.

"Doctor Parker," the general continued, "will need an escort to the Xathi crash site in order to investigate some interesting readings her machinery has been picking up."

I turned back to him. "Why wasn't team one given this assignment? They interact with the humans more, have experience with them."

His look was not happy. He made his way around his desk as he spoke. "Not that I need to explain myself to you, but you would have known this if you hadn't exiled yourself. Vrehx and Jeneva are expecting. Due to the sensitive nature of this child being the first human-

Skotan mix, Vrehx will temporarily be held back until the child is born."

"Then send another team, sir. Let Sk'lar and his men be her bodyguard."

Rouhr took one large step towards me. I could feel the heat of his breath as he snarled at me. "You are an insolent, disrespectful fool. I chose your team, and you presume to think you can tell me otherwise?"

I did not move. I turned my head to look him in the eyes. "I do not wish to waste my time as a babysitter for some dirt-collector, sir."

"I'm not a 'dirt-collector,'" I heard her say, fury in her tone, but I ignored her.

The general and I stared at one another for what seemed like many long minutes. I could hear the men shuffling their feet behind me. I had no intention of breaking, but when he smiled, I somehow knew things would not go well for me.

"You, my old friend, truly are a fool," he said as he kept staring at me. His words were calm and whispered. "*You* have decided to turn your back on your team, your crew, and me. *You* have decided to place yourself into exile in order to search for a way off this planet and back to our world. While I do not dismiss the necessity of your search, I do not believe in the obsession behind it."

I opened my mouth to challenge his statement, but

his words came faster. "You are the one that has chosen to become this person that you are now. So, I present you with a choice. You will take this assignment and complete it in the manner in which you complete all of your missions, or you will resign your commission."

"Then I resign, sir."

"Ah, you should truly let me finish." A smile split his face, and it wasn't friendly in the least. "If I accept your resignation, you will no longer be allowed to use the *Aurora,* live on the *Aurora,* or have contact with the *Aurora,* since it is currently a military installation. You will be a civilian, without military access and without military privilege." He stepped away from me and walked over to the human woman. "Now, old friend. What is your decision?"

At the moment, I disliked the general immensely. To blackmail me into working this assignment was beneath him. It was juvenile, and petty.

But I needed the *Aurora* and her computers.

I nodded, not trusting my own voice to be civil at that moment.

He clapped his hands and rubbed them together. "Good. Doctor Parker, you have already been introduced to the others, and while this is certainly not the introduction I had wanted, I would like to introduce to you Commander Karzin, leader of Strike

Team Two, and normally a more reasonable person than now."

She nodded, looking as though she would walk towards me, then thought better of it. "Thank you, General."

"What exactly will we be investigating, sir?" I asked.

The general turned the floor over to the woman, who looked at me, but made a point to look at the others as well. "My sensors have been picking up seismic activity at the Xathi crash site, something that has not happened before. I am being sent to look into it, take samples, and ensure that the sensors are working properly."

"Fine. I assume we're leaving soon?" I asked.

Again, she was the one to answer. "As soon as you're ready to go, Commander."

I grunted, and turned to leave.

The sooner this babysitting assignment was over, the sooner I could get back to my real job.

Finding a way home.

ANNIE

If someone had told me I'd be spending my afternoon sandwiched between two giant aliens as we sped off to the middle of the desert, I would've said they were insane.

When I reported the tremors to the head of the lab, I never expected they would send me to General Rouhr on my own. The stories in the news painted him as some kind of fearless and fearsome warrior. While there was no doubt in my mind that he fit that description, I didn't expect him to be as polite and kind as he was. I found I wasn't scared of him at all.

The glaring Valorni sitting beside me, on the other hand, I *was* a little scared of. My arms were tucked into my sides as close to my body as possible. I didn't want to bump him by accident. The scowl on his face had remained in place from the moment he entered General Rouhr's office until now.

If he hadn't been so determined to frown, he'd have been almost handsome. And there was no doubt that his broad frame was intriguing.

And I'd happily stare and touch him if he hadn't been glowering the whole time.

As my mind focused on what the Valorni would look like without a scowl, my arm suddenly brushed his.

Electric sparks shot through my body as he turned to look at me.

Startled, I removed my arm again. He stared at me for a long moment before looking away.

This was one angry alien.

That whole argument between the Valorni and General Rouhr was unsettling. I wasn't sure how I felt about being escorted by a team with a leader that seemed to want nothing to do with me.

The general also mentioned something about an intervention. I wondered if putting this…Strike Team Two on my case was part of that intervention. I couldn't say I was pleased to be dragged into what sounded like quite personal problems, but as long as I got to look at my equipment and figure out what those tremors were, I didn't care.

Still, by the look of the Valorni's face, this little excursion was a major inconvenience for him. He came off as an asshole in General Rouhr's office, but my mother had always taught me to be polite and considerate of others.

That applied even to the grouchy Valorni.

"If I'm pulling you away from a more important assignment, I apologize," I said, though I couldn't imagine anything more important than this. "I didn't anticipate your general would assemble a whole team to escort me."

"Karzin? More important assignments?" One of the other aliens, a Skotan, chuckled. "That's quite humorous."

"Do you like your teeth, Rokul?" The glowering Valorni, Karzin, snapped. "Keep talking and I'll make them into a windchime for you to hang in front of your door." The Skotan, Rokul, snorted but didn't say anything more.

There was clearly some tension in this group, but that was completely uncalled for. I turned to face Karzin head on.

"If I'd known your general was going to send me out to the desert, I would've insisted on picking escorts that were actually willing to go," I told him.

"I can't imagine anyone that would be willing to go

poke about in a desert collecting grains of sand," Karzin snapped.

That was the second time he'd insulted my profession, this time it was to my face. I wasn't going to put up with this for the rest of the day.

"It's not my fault you can't grasp the concept of geology," I replied. "Don't blame me for your ignorance."

A heavy silence settled over the transport unit. Karzin stared me down, no doubt expecting me to cower under his steely gaze. To be honest, I wanted to, but if I did, he'd feel free to be a pain in the ass for the rest of this excursion. I wasn't prepared to deal with that.

To my surprise, he tipped his head back and laughed.

"The rock lady has a backbone!" he laughed. "How refreshing."

The tension in the carrier evaporated. I hadn't expected him to react in that way. I didn't have any clue how I was supposed to respond.

Karzin didn't seem to care.

"So, rock lady, answer me this," he continued. "General Rouhr introduced you as Annie, but that fancy key card around your neck says Andromeda. Which is it?"

"I prefer to go by Annie," I explained.

"But your real name is Andromeda?"

"Yes," I nodded.

"I'm going to call you Andromeda," Karzin said decidedly.

"Prepare to be ignored then," I replied.

"What's so wrong with Andromeda?" Karzin asked.

I didn't respond. I felt childish, but I had the sense that with Karzin, if I gave him an inch, he'd take a mile. He reminded me of Cassie in that way, but all comparisons stopped there. A small, twisted part of me wanted to see what would happen if Cassie and Karzin went head to head in an argument.

"I don't like it," I finally replied.

"Why not?"

"Do I need to have a reason?" I answered. "I simply prefer to go by Annie."

"Whatever you say, Andromeda," Karzin smirked.

Jerk.

I folded my arms across my chest and looked away, making a show of ignoring him. Unbelievable. I'd known him for all of five minutes and he was making me, a grown woman, pout like a child.

I told myself that everything was fine. I just had to deal with him for this one assignment. Once I recovered my data, I could retreat to my lab and do some real work for once.

"Hey, Andromeda," he said. I ignored him.

"Andromeda," he repeated. I continued to ignore him,

"Annie!"

"Yes?" I replied.

"I think I might know what caused your sensors to go off the charts," Karzin said. He was looking out the window. I leaned past his massive body in an attempt to see what he was talking about. Below us, the landscape was dotted with pieces of the fallen Xathi ship. Right in the middle of the fallout area was a massive, perfectly circular crater.

"What the fuck is that?" I gasped. "That wasn't there before."

"You don't say," Karzin commented. "Mystery solved then?"

"No." I settled back down in my seat. "Mystery far from solved. I don't know what it's like where you come from, but pieces of the planet don't just collapse here."

Something cold flitted through his gaze but was gone before I could fully comprehend it.

The pilot of our transport unit set us down as close to the edge of the crater as he dared. Karzin was the first to leap out of the unit. I quickly followed after him.

"What's the plan here, Andromeda?" he asked.

I walked by him without a word, but heard him laugh softly behind me as he followed.

“Were any of you in the area when the pieces of the Xathi ship fell here?” I asked.

“We all were,” a K’ver responded.

“Oh,” I said quietly. “Well, does anything look different?”

“Aside from the hole?” Karzin asked.

“Yes, aside from the hole,” I nodded.

“Nothing stands out,” Karzin replied. “I’d have to see the original pictures taken of the area to tell you for sure.” He shaded his eyes. “We were all pretty busy with the battle.”

Oh. Of course they were.

Not all of the Xathi had been killed when their ship crashed. The strike teams had taken care of any survivors.

“I can examine the photos myself when I get back to the lab,” I said. I stepped up to the crater, the toes of my boots inches from the edge. I slowly leaned forward, peering into the depths of the crater.

“See anything?” Karzin’s voice startled me. I hadn’t realized he was standing so close.

“Are you trying to kill me?” I snapped.

“I would’ve caught you if you tumbled forward,” he said with a dismissive wave.

“Like I’m going to trust you,” I grumbled.

“You should. I’m in charge of your well-being,” he replied.

"That doesn't make me feel any better."

Karzin stepped up next to me and peered in. I was tempted to startle him, but I didn't want to stoop to his level.

"Looks deep," he commented. He took something out of his pocket, a clear vial of some sort. He clicked the button on the top of the vial and it suddenly began to glow. He tossed it into the crater. Together, we watched it fall until it was completely swallowed by darkness.

"I'm going to send a probe down," I announced. I walked back to the transport unit for one of my supply packs. The silver probe was remotely operated and could change its orientation so that it could embed itself at any angle. I returned to the lip of the crater and deployed it.

"What will that do?" Karzin asked.

"I'm going to send it down as far as I can and stick it into the side of the crater. It will collect information and give us a better idea of what's going on here," I explained.

"I didn't know you needed so many fancy gadgets to look at dirt," Karzin said.

"Says the one carrying glowsticks," I scoffed.

"Those are useful survival tools," Karzin replied.

"That's a shame. Now yours is at the bottom of a chasm. Won't be very useful to you now." The probe reached maximum depth, about a half mile below the surface. I reoriented it so it could bury its spike in the crater wall. After a few moments, data started pouring to my portable console.

"Interesting," I mumbled.

"Are you going to share with the rest of us or are you going to keep us in suspense?" Karzin asked.

"From the lip of the crater inward, the planet's crust is unusually thin," I said.

"I could've told you that," Karzin said, gesturing to the gaping hole.

"Can you tell me why the planetary crust is thinner in this specific area?" I looked at him expectantly.

"No," Karzin admitted. "Can the probe?"

"It can give me clues," I explained. "The probe is telling me that this specific area has always been thinner than the surrounding area, it didn't recently degrade into this state. The fact that it's perfectly circular tells me that this didn't occur naturally. The impact of the Xathi ship pieces probably cracked the thin crust. A slight shift in the tectonic plates would've been enough to make this whole thing collapse."

I looked up at Karzin. His mouth was open, he looked like he was struggling to come up with a quip. When he didn't say anything, I kept going.

"The probe can't tell me much more than that. It

can't collect samples for me, either, so I'm going into the crater."

"I'm sorry, what?" Karzin blinked in surprise.

"I misspoke," I corrected. "We're going into the crater."

KARZIN

"I misspoke, we're going into the crater."

I had not anticipated that. I'd found her slightly interesting when she stood up to me and defended herself.

I found it even more intriguing to learn that our pretty, prickly Annie Parker was Andromeda Parker and how much she hated her name.

This, though, this took me by surprise.

She had said she was going into the crater, changed it to '*we* are going into the crater', then immediately turned around to get her gear. The others were flitting their glances between her and me, amusement when they looked at me, pride and admiration when they looked at her.

Fine. If she wanted to rappel down, we would

rappel down. "Rokul, you're going down with us." If he wanted to make snide comments about me, then the least he could do was fall down a hole with me. "The rest of you will be our lookouts and carry the slack. Gear up."

I was happy to see the team respond without comment or hesitation. It wasn't long before the three of us were geared up, hooked up, and looking over the edge of the crater. "You ready, Andromeda?" I asked as I looked at her.

She was good at ignoring me, but I could see a small vein in her neck throbbing. She really hated her name.

"You ready?" I asked again.

She looked up at me, winked, and said "Watch me," as she went over the edge. Iq'her was working her line and was almost caught by surprise with her sudden departure. I shook my head and chuckled to myself. She had guts.

Rokul was next, his brother handling his line. I followed them down, knowing Sylor would take care of my line no matter how angry he was at me.

It was plain to see that Annie was enjoying herself. I just couldn't see how. It was dirt, rocks, sand, and more dirt. Sure, some of it was a different color and consistency than the rest, but it was still dirt. While I hung there, I picked up a small rock and looked at it. It wasn't actually a rock, it was small sheets of rock stuck together. It broke apart easily and barely had any weight to it.

"That's called shale," I heard her say. I looked over to see her watching me.

"Shale. Huh. Did you need a sample?"

She nodded, then reached into one of her pouches. She pulled out a small bag and showed me how to label it after I put the shale inside of it. She then bounced over to Rokul and had him do the same. I was picking rock and dirt out of a crater and putting it into small baggies. This is what my missions had been reduced to.

"Don't skip any parts, get me samples from as many types of soil as you can," she called out to us.

I looked around. "It all looks the same. Look, it's gray here, it's gray over there," I pointed to my right, "and it's gray down here," I finished with a light kick to the crater wall.

She fluttered her lips with a big exhale. "It might look the same to untrained eyes, but I promise you, that's all different. Each layer of dirt and rock tells a story." Her voice became gentle, almost serene as she spoke. This was where she wanted to be, it was easy to see.

"You see, each planet is made up of billions and billions of layers of rock, dirt, and sediment, and each layer tells a different story. If it's compressed together like that shale," she pointed at the section I was dangling on a level with. "Then something was happening at the time that forced the dirt down on itself with such heat and pressure that it essentially glued itself together." With a wave she gestured to another level. "The parts where it's looser, that means the planet was potentially experiencing a more humid period that allowed the dirt to stay lose and fertile."

"Each layer is a page in the history book of this planet. Even if they look the same, each story is different. Each story is a chance to learn something about this planet that we never knew before." I watched as she dangled in the air, looking at the crater walls in admiration and joy. I still only saw dirt and rocks, but I had more appreciation for what she was doing. To find something that gave you that kind of feeling, that kind of joy, it was something to admire.

We went lower to collect more samples and to get closer to the probe she'd dropped earlier. "So, what could be the story for the dirt here?" Rokul asked as he rappelled down next to her. I stayed a little higher up, still working on getting a particularly difficult rock out.

"I won't know until I get around to testing it. It could be anything. We're actually still trying to figure out how old this planet is, so it could be anything from an ice age to a time when the world was too hot to live on." She stopped talking and took a closer look at the section she was at.

As I came down next to her, I asked. "What is it?"

"I don't know," she answered. "This section here makes no sense to me. See this here?" she asked as she pointed.

I looked, and what I saw was a solid piece of multi-colored rock. It had at least eight different shades of green mixed in with another nine or ten shades of brown.

"This shouldn't be here. Everything around it is soft in comparison, but this layer is as solid as can be and extremely colorful."

She took out her pick and hammer, set the pick to the rock, and hit it. The noise that reverberated around the crater was loud. Both Rokul and I were forced to cover our ears, while Annie grimaced through it. We looked back at the rock and there was no indication that she had hit it. "That makes no sense," she said.

"Any ideas?" I asked her.

She shook her head. "No, nothing. Does this run around the entire crater?"

I flicked on my radio to the team above. "Takar? Sylor? Rokul and I are going to make our way around the crater a few hundred feet. Monitor our lines."

"Aye, sir," Sylor answered. I nodded to Rokul and we made our way around the crater in opposite directions. For me, the rock line was the same for the entire hundred-plus feet that I traveled.

"Heading back, Sylor." He grunted in response as he took up the slack while I headed back to Annie's position. "Same, the entire way until I stopped."

"That's interesting," she whispered, more to herself than to me. Rokul returned a moment later to report the same. "That makes me wonder. Could there have been a catastrophic, planet-changing event during this time?"

"How long ago do you think this was?" Rokul asked.

"That's a good question. Let's see, we're about five hundred feet down, each layer is between one-and-a-half to seven centimeters thick..." We waited for a minute or two as she tried to do the calculations in her head. "To be honest, I'm not completely sure, because the gravity level is different here than on Earth, not by a lot, but enough to make a difference. I'd say that this could have been anywhere from six hundred to a thousand years ago, but don't quote me on that. It's something I need to run by some of my coworkers." She looked, first at Rokul, then over to me. "Let's go a little lower, get a few more samples."

Over the course of the next three hours, we dropped another two hundred feet, gathering samples along the way. The sun had moved, and it was getting to be too dark to see on my side of the crater. I pulled out a light stick and flicked it on, but as I went to attach it to my waist, something hit my hand. I watched as the light stick fell until it was too dark for me to see it anymore.

What in the skrell was that? "Rokul?"

"Sir?"

"Get out a light stick, see if you can see anything."

"I actually still have light in my section, sir."

Of all the...I took a deep breath, let it out slowly, and calmed myself down. "Then come over here where the light is gone and light up a ketonsin light stick." Okay, maybe I hadn't calmed down.

"Yes, sir," I heard him say quietly. He made his way over to me, lit up a light stick, and, as he went to pass it to me, something knocked it from his hands. "What in the...?" he didn't get to finish his sentence as something struck him, sending him spinning away from me.

"Rokul!" Then I head Annie scream and saw her being tossed around on her wire. Before I could move, something started hitting me on the legs, then the arms.

We were all yelling, screaming, and grunting as we tried to defend ourselves from our mystery attackers. I lashed out and hit something with my hand that felt slimy and hard. "Get us up!" I yelled into my comm, then Annie's scream changed the direction of my focus. She was being spun around and batted against the walls relentlessly.

Rokul was already making his way up, his line tight as his brother pulled. I started to make my way to

Annie when I was suddenly jerked upwards. “No, no. She’s in trouble! Let me back down,” I ordered.

“Make up your ketonsin mind, please,” Sylor shot back. I made my way over towards Annie, but was tripped along the way and sent into a nauseating spin. I finally got to her, attached my emergency line to her, and detached her from her line just as it broke.

“PULL!” we both yelled. We started to rise, and as I kicked at something trying to wrap around my foot, I looked into Annie’s eyes.

The need to comfort the terror I found there was overwhelming. I pulled her fragile body closer into mine, to protect and shelter her. The movement highlighted the swell of her breasts pressed to my chest.

With her scent, with the feel of her heartbeat, for a moment I forgot the Xathi. I forgot the war. I forgot the satellites.

I forgot everything but her, and simply enjoyed the moment.

I shook my head violently. She was a human, and it was her kind ruining the crew. I wouldn’t let her ruin me.

ANNIE

I collapsed into my seat on the transport unit. My heart still raced. I looked down at my hands, forcing myself to take slow, steady breaths.

I wasn't aware of Karzin and the rest of Strike Team Two as they climbed into their seats. It wasn't until the transport unit was off the ground that everyone started talking.

"Did anyone see what attacked us?" Karzin asked.

"I couldn't see anything," Rokul replied. "It was too dark."

"We couldn't see anything, either," Sylor added. "I just saw the ropes start to jerk and swing and knew you had to be pulled up."

"Thank you," I said quietly.

Sylor offered me a reassuring smile.

"What could it have been?" Karzin asked me.

I simply shook my head.

"I don't know. It could've been debris falling off the crater walls. We were in the dark. It's possible we were jumping at shadows, so to speak," I said.

"I don't think so," Karzin insisted. "Those strikes were deliberate. There was no noise before the first strike, either. If it was debris, we would've heard it clattering down."

"I guess you'd know better than I would," I admitted. "My specialty is rocks. Rocks don't usually attack people."

"Usually?" Karzin chuckled softly.

I tried to laugh back, but the action caused my muscles to spasm painfully.

"Are you all right?" Karzin asked quickly.

"Whatever it was struck me in the back," I said.

"Let me have a look," Karzin offered. Something about our misadventure had flipped a switch with him. With us.

As I shrugged off my jacket, I thought about the way he'd looked at me as I clung to him. As annoyed as I was with him before we went into the crater, I was glad he was here now. The strength that had emanated from him was nearly enough to make me lose my grip on reality.

Now that I was in just my tank top, I turned my

back to him. I felt his fingers lightly graze my shoulders and the less tender areas of my back. I felt goosebumps rise on my arms. I hadn't felt this sensation in years, but I recognized it as the beginnings of attraction.

It's the adrenaline, nothing more, I scolded myself as Karzin examined me.

"You already have a nasty bruise forming," he said. "You're going to be feeling that for a while."

"I could've told you that." I echoed his joke from earlier.

"Very funny," he chuckled. "Are you sure you're okay?"

"I'm fine," I insisted. "Just in pain."

Karzin withdrew his hands and I tugged my jacket back on.

"I know a fantastic doctor," Karzin said brightly. The others lifted their heads, as if they knew exactly who Karzin was talking about. "She'll see you if she knows you're with us. You don't even have to make an appointment."

"I appreciate the thought, but I can't pay for a doctor right now," I said.

"Who said anything about paying?" Karzin looked confused. "Dr. Parr is paid by General Rouhr. Anyone who works for him gets free access to her services. You officially work for him now."

"I don't think I do," I shook my head.

"You're going to be until we get to the bottom of whatever is in that crater," Karzin argued. "I'm taking you to see Dr. Parr."

I felt that it was pointless to argue, and my back really did hurt.

"Okay," I agreed.

"Glad to see you can be reasonable, Andromeda," Karzin smirked.

I rolled my eyes. "At least one of us can."

When we reached Nyheim, Karzin helped me out of the carrier. I winced when my feet came into contact with the ground. Pain shot through my entire body.

"We'll take it slow," Karzin assured me. He asked the members of his strike team to ensure my equipment was unloaded and returned to the proper place. I hadn't even thought of that.

At first, I tried to walk on my own, but sitting still in the transport unit had actually made my back feel so much worse. When we first climbed out of the crater, I'd felt like I could manage. Now, every step was agony.

"Do you need me to carry you?" Karzin offered. I couldn't tell if he was serious or not.

"I'm fine," I winced.

"No, you're not. At least give me your arm. Put some weight on me." Karzin offered his arm. I wove mine through his and leaned on him. My palm rested on the part of his skin that was green. My fingers draped over one of the purple bands that wrapped around his arms.

I let my mind rest on how different his skin felt. It was harder. And the texture was slightly different where his stripes were. So unlike the fragile skin I wore as a human. His was built to withstand assault. He was built for battle.

After a few steps, he looked down at me and smiled.

"You can put more weight on me than that you know. I can take it."

"I'm putting half my weight on you as it is," I replied.

Karzin blinked in surprise.

"If that's true, then it's amazing how a strong wind hasn't blown you away yet," he chuckled.

"You realize you're the abnormal one here, right?" I laughed. "I'm barely shorter than average. You, on the other hand, tower over almost everyone."

"Then it's amazing how your entire population hasn't blown away on a strong gust of wind," he amended.

I shook my head.

"Don't make me laugh," I warned him. "It hurts to laugh. Can you go back to being a pain in the ass?"

"I'm never a pain in the ass," he said facetiously. His face grew grim. "However, I can apologize to you for not doing my job."

"What?" I looked up at him, confused.

"General Rouhr asked me to keep you safe. I didn't do that," he explained.

"I'm alive, aren't I? I think you met the basic requirement of the job."

"One doesn't become a strike team leader by meeting the basic requirements," he mumbled.

"Are strike team leaders supposed to anticipate attacks from unseen forces?" I asked.

"Yes, actually," Karzin said.

Oh.

I wasn't sure what to say next. We walked in silence until we reached a pristine white medical office. Karzin walked right through the waiting room. No one was inclined to stop him. He took me to a room at the end of the hall filled with six hospital beds and a woman who looked a little too young to be a doctor.

"Evie, I brought you a present," Karzin called.

The woman looked up from her clipboard and stared at Karzin like she'd seen a ghost.

"I didn't know you were back," she smiled.

"I'm not. Not really," Karzin said awkwardly. Silence hung between them for a moment before he turned his attention to me. "This is Annie. She was injured on an assignment. I told her you'd fix her up."

"I'd be happy to." She took my free arm and Karzin released me.

"I'm going to report what happened to General Rouhr," he told me. "I'll see you later."

"See you," I said. I watched him leave the room before turning to the woman.

"I'm Dr. Parr." She guided me to the nearest bed, monitoring how I walked. "Call me Evie. I used to patch Karzin and the other strike teams up all the time. What happened?"

"We went out to where the pieces of the Xathi ship fell back down to the planet's surface," I began. "I'm a geologist. General Rouhr sent me to investigate serious tremors my equipment picked up. When we got out there, there was a huge crater. While we were rappelling into it, something attacked us." I removed my jacket and showed her my bruise.

"Whatever it was, it was strong," she murmured. "Do you remember anything about it?"

"Nothing," I sighed. "I never saw it. It struck so fast. I didn't even realize I was hurt until Karzin got me out of the crater. I thought it might've been debris from the crater wall, but Karzin insists it was a deliberate attack. I hate to admit it, but I'm inclined to agree with him. It felt alive."

As I spoke, Evie cleaned and sanitized my back. There were a few small cuts in addition to the bruising.

"What did the impact feel like?" She filled a syringe

with clear liquid. "You're going to feel a little pinch," she warned.

"It felt like I got the wind knocked out of me. And it stung." I winced as the needle impaled the flesh of my arm. Within a few moments, a warm tingly sensation spread throughout my body. The sharp pains gave away to a dull, throbbing sensation that wasn't painful, just odd.

"There are a few scrapes on your back. It looks like you're having a minor reaction to whatever you came into contact with," she explained.

"I swear, I have no idea what it could be," I repeated.

Evie placed a gentle hand on my shoulder and smiled reassuringly.

"I believe you. Unfortunately, I have no idea what it could be, either." She grabbed a datapad and plugged in a few notes. "I'm going to give you something for the pain. I don't detect any breaks or fractures, but the bruising is deep. You're going to need a painkiller if you want to function like a normal human being."

"Yes, I need to function like a normal human," I laughed.

"If you want to look deeper into what was in that crater, I might be able to point you in the right direction," Evie offered. "I'm sending you home with instructions for how to take care of yourself while your body recovers. I'm also going to include the contact information for a friend of mine. Her name is Jeneva. She's the one to talk to about weird stuff happening on the planet. She lived in the jungle alone for over a decade before the Xathi invasion. She's seen stuff no one else has ever seen before."

"Jeneva," I repeated. Why did the name sound so familiar? "Wait, I heard General Rouhr mention her name. She's married to one of the aliens, isn't she?"

"That's right," Evie said brightly. "Definitely give her a call if you're feeling up to it."

"I will." I nodded. "Thank you."

Evie sent me off with a bottle of pills and a list of instructions. As I left her clinic, feeling pain in every step, I wished I'd asked Karzin to wait for me.

KARZIN

I left Annie in Evie's capable hands and made my way to the general's office. Evie's clinic was only a few buildings away, so it wasn't much of a walk. Tobias was there to greet me again.

"Karzin!" his voice rang through the halls at a pitch that should have threatened the windows. "I see that you've come back from your mission. It's so good to see you healthy and in one piece, sir."

"Is the general in?" I asked. I ignored the rest of his overenthusiastic exuberance, or at least I tried to.

"Of course, of course. I'll take you to him," he practically sang out as he stepped away from his desk.

I held up my hands to stop him. "No, no, it is all right. I know where his office is. I think I can make it there on my own."

His face never changed. He must have been the most positive, peppy person in the history of humankind. "Oh, I know that, sir. But I enjoy the walk and it's my job. Besides," he said in a painfully higher pitch, then his voice dropped to a nearly impossible bass compared to what his voice was before. "It's my job."

With my mind still reeling from the surprising vocal antics, I followed him in silence to the general's office. When Tobias opened the door, his smile and pep were back, as was the cheerfully high pitch to his voice. "Here you go. He's already expecting you."

As I walked past him, he smiled at me, then closed the door behind me. I looked at the general, who was looking at paperwork on his desk. "That Tobias is an interesting fellow," I said quietly.

The general looked up, slight confusion, then recognition, lighting his face. "That he is, but you have to love his upbeat personality."

"'Upbeat' is nowhere near the word for him. Have you heard him when he's not upbeat?"

"Ahh, you're talking about his real voice," he said with a knowing nod. "He lost everyone and everything in the attack. He was hiding in a hole as the Xathi killed his family, so I think he's trying to be overly exuberant as a way to cope."

He motioned for me to sit. I took the seat he indicated. I waited until he'd cleaned up the paperwork he was looking at, stacking it neatly at the corner of his desk, an extravagant desk by the general's standards aboard the *Vengeance*.

He saw me looking at the desk and looked embarrassed. "It was one of the few desks that survived the initial attack here in Nyheim and Vidia wanted me to have something a little more posh. I know it's not my style, but it is nice. She says it's important for making an impression."

"It certainly is, sir," I responded. The desk was well built, made of a dark wood with a light wood used for the accents. I found myself liking it, as well, and glad that the general had something besides a simple metal table to work at for a change.

Maybe there was something good to Vidia. Maybe.

"Report. What did you find?"

I repositioned myself in my chair, then told him. "Things were fine as long as the sun was providing our light, but as soon as it became too dark to see and we broke out the light sticks, that's when the attack happened."

"And none of you got a look at what was attacking you?"

"No, sir. The only thing I remember was that it was strong, had a slimy coating, and was fast. I punched it, or at least thought I did, and it did nothing."

He steepled his hands in front of him and let out a deep breath. "Okay. Where is Doctor Parker now?"

"I dropped her off with Dr. Parr," I answered. "Annie had a fairly nasty bruise on her back, so I thought it would be prudent to get her to Evie for a checkup."

"Good. Do you think that whatever attacked you in the crater could be responsible for the crater?"

I shook my head, not as a negative, but as an admission of ignorance. "I wouldn't be able to tell you, sir. Since we didn't get a look at whatever it was, or they were, I couldn't say with certainty."

"That doesn't make me feel better."

"My apologies, sir."

He sat back, folded his arms on his chest, and looked around the room. "Very well. we have a crater that was caused by some seismic activity that could or could not have been caused by whatever attacked you down there. Whatever attacked you must have felt threatened in some way, but I wonder if they were threatened by your light or by you."

I hadn't thought of that.

"The only thing that I believe we can count as good in this situation is that this crater is nowhere near civilization."

"That is true, General. However, it's not far from the *Aurora*," I said.

"Yes, which brings me to something you won't be happy with."

I felt a combination of dread and fury rising up inside me. He was going to evacuate us, I just knew he was. It was the prudent thing to do.

"I believe that the best thing to do at the moment is for you to stay closer, at least until we know if this is an isolated incident or not." He leaned forward. "I know this is an inconvenience," he started.

"Do you know how long?" I asked. "I was doing important work on the ship."

The general cleared his throat before answering. "I understand that, but I would rather play it safe with this new threat. Once it's over, you're free to go back to your…duties."

"That means I, as well, will need a new place to stay, sir." I was not happy. The *Aurora* had been my home since the *Vengeance* was destroyed. Where was I to stay?

I would rather have taken my chances on the ship, but the general was right. It was better to be safe.

"I'm sorry, Karzin. It is only temporary, I promise."

"Aye, sir." I finished up the rest of my report to the general, then left. I needed to find somewhere to stay until this situation was figured out and handled, and I didn't want to ask any of the team.

As I left the office, I saw Annie walking my way from Dr. Parr's. "Salutations, Andromeda!"

She rolled her eyes as she acknowledged me with a partial wave.

"How are you, Annie?"

Was that a small smile on her face as I used her chosen name instead of her real one? Possibly.

And I rather liked it.

She answered me. "I'm okay, just in pain."

"The adrenaline has worn off. You're going to be sore for a while. Did Evie give you anything for the pain?"

She nodded. "Yeah, she did. She's great, so happy and polite. She's fantastic. How did your report go?"

"Not as well as I had hoped. In addition to having many more questions and not a lot of answers, General Rouhr has asked me to stay closer."

She looked up at me, tilting her neck at an almost absurd angle. "Does that mean you need to find a place to stay? Sorry," she apologized as I made a face. "I sort of overheard the others before you got there saying you were staying on another ship."

"They're right, I do live there, or at least I did." We started walking down the street. "Hungry?" I asked.

"Famished, but I don't have the money," she admitted.

"I didn't ask if you did," I said to her. I took her to a nearby café that I knew and ordered both of us something to eat and drink.

"Thank you," she said after her first bite.

"I figured you would need to replenish your strength, and the medicines that Evie gives usually work better with a full stomach," I answered her.

She nodded and mumbled something through a mouth full of food. I stifled a laugh and hid my amusement by taking a bite of my own food.

"What are you thinking about?"

I looked up to see Annie looking at me. Her curiosity was evident.

I finished my glass of iced tea, one of the things I could honestly say that the humans had done well. It was very tasty and refreshing, and I requested a refill. I turned my attention back to Annie. "I was just thinking of where to go. Many of the neighborhoods and towns are still uneasy about having an alien around. And... there aren't many places with the teams where I would be welcome, not with how I've been acting lately," I admitted.

With a tilt of her head, Annie looked at me as she ate a fried potato stick. "I might know of a place."

"Really?"

"Yeah. It's where I live, a small place called Somerst, maybe a mile or two from the city limits," she explained. "There's a small boarding house there. It's not the greatest place, but it's solid. The owner is pretty nice, and she could use the money. Actually," she added quietly, "the whole town needs the money."

"I'd be willing to take a look at it," I said. When Annie smiled, I actually felt glad to see her do so.

She had been hurt on my watch, and that was something I did not take well to. To see her smile meant she was okay.

And it was lovely.

I returned her smile with one of my own. A genuine smile.

We stood there, smiling at each other. She twirled her hair as her eyes danced. I stood like a fool.

Yet somehow it just felt…right.

ANNIE

"Shit!" I grabbed Karzin's arm before he boarded the shuttle.

"What's wrong? Are you hurt?" His eyes scanned my body looking for signs of injury.

"I was supposed to go the market," I groaned. In all of the excitement, I had completely forgotten. My family expected me home hours ago. I couldn't believe that it was only this morning that I yelled at Cassie for taking too long in the shower.

"Is it still open?" he asked. I checked my watch.

"For another hour."

"Let's go, then," Karzin walked off in the direction of the market before I could convince him otherwise. I hobbled after him. I'd already taken one of the pills Dr. Parr prescribed for me. It took care of most of the pain.

Karzin realized I was a few paces behind him and stopped to wait for me.

"Can you make it?" he asked.

"I'm banged up, but I'm not completely useless," I joked.

I walked directly behind Karzin, relying on his broad form to part the crowd. Quite a few of Nyheim's citizens blatantly stared at his appearance, nearly stumbling over their own feet to get out of his way. No one noticed me trailing behind him.

Thanks to Karzin, it only took us ten minutes to walk to the open market. On a normal day at this time, I would've been fighting crowds for at least twenty minutes.

"I'm going to hire you to walk in front of me from now on," I joked.

"You can't afford me," Karzin smirked.

"Do I get a discount if you don't have to talk?" I replied.

"It costs extra to shut me up," he quipped.

I rolled my eyes and made an attempt to step around him, but immediately came into contact with the shoulder of another marketgoer. Ordinarily, that wouldn't have done much, but this time it sent a shockwave through my body that made me stumble. Karzin steadied me with one hand and gave the man who'd bumped me a nasty look.

"It's fine," I muttered. "It's normal in the market."

"It's not fine when you're injured," Karzin replied. "Stay behind me and point me in the right direction." He gently pushed me behind him and bid me to hold on to one of his belt loops. I felt like a troublesome child being led about.

"I need bread," I called to him over the din of the busy market. Karzin began walking, cutting a path wherever he stepped. I stared at his back as we walked. He wasn't doing anything more than walking, but with each step, his muscles shifted beneath the fabric of his shirt.

I knew little about the Valorni race, but I'd heard they were excellent warriors. I pitied anything that had to fight Karzin on the battlefield.

When he stopped, I slammed into his back. It was like running into a building.

"We're at the bread stand," he announced.

"You could've given me a heads up," I stepped around him to examine the bread for sale. There wasn't much left. I took a dark loaf identical to the one Cassie and Helix finished off this morning.

Karzin lead me from stand to stand until I had two big bags filled with everything I needed. He carried both bags while I followed in his wake. The shuttle station was even more crowded when we returned.

Thankfully, he cut a figure so intimidating, people stood aside to allow him to board.

"It's convenient to travel with you," I said to him once we found seats. "Are you sure you can't give me a discount for your services?"

"Since you're hurt, you get the first day free," Karzin smiled.

"How generous." I reached into one of the market bags and pulled out an apple. "Take one," I urged him as I pulled a second one out for myself.

"Isn't this for your family?"

"I bought a couple extra," I explained. "It'll go bad if not eaten."

"What is it?" he asked, turning over the red fruit.

"It's an apple. You've been here months and you haven't seen an apple yet?" I asked.

"I guess not," Karzin shrugged before devouring half of the apple in one bite. "It's sweet!" he exclaimed.

I didn't hold back my laughter as I watched him finish the rest of it, core and all.

"Most people don't eat that bit," I told him.

"I'm not people." He flashed a grin.

The shuttle came to a stop just outside of town. Karzin balanced the bags on his arms as I followed him off the shuttle. Less than twenty people disembarked with us. Karzin stopped to take in the site of Somerst.

I hated myself for it, but when I looked at the

mismatched buildings and dirt roads, I felt a pang of embarrassment. Maybe I should've told Karzin more about Somerst beforehand.

"I understand if you'd rather not stay here," I said quietly.

"Why wouldn't I?" he asked. "You're kind enough to help me find a place to stay and I'm intelligent enough to accept your offer. I just didn't realize how little the new settlements had."

"We get by," I replied. "It's not as rough as it looks." I motioned for him to follow me as I started off down the main, and only, road.

"That's my house there." I pointed to my home. A light was on in the window. I could see the shadows of my family.

"How many live with you?" Karzin asked.

"I live with my parents and both of my siblings," I answered.

"In that small space?" Karzin said in disbelief.

"We make it work," I shrugged. "I'm just grateful we have a roof over our heads, especially since my older brother was injured fighting the Xathi in Duvest."

"I'm sorry we couldn't prevent it," Karzin said, his voice sounding far away and angry.

"I don't blame you," I said quickly. "If it weren't for you and the rest of your team, we'd all be dead."

We moved past my home in silence and didn't speak again until I stopped in front of the boarding house.

"It's not much," I said. "But there's clean sheets and fresh water. Finola might give you a hard time when you come in, but she won't squawk too much once she realizes you're a paying customer."

"I think I can handle it," Karzin replied.

"You say that now but you haven't met Finola. She lived in Einhiv when the hybrids overtook the city. I didn't see it myself, but someone said they saw her punch one right in the face without a hint of fear in her eyes," I told him.

"Impressive. If it's true," Karzin nodded.

"Once you meet her, you'll know it's true," I laughed. Karzin and I lingered outside the crooked boarding house door. I was glad I had taken the market bags from him, I wouldn't have known what to do with my hands otherwise.

"Well," I cleared my throat. "Let me know if General Rouhr wants to do anything about whatever that thing was in the crater."

"Certainly," Karzin nodded.

I turned to leave, not knowing what else to say, but I didn't take even a step before I realized I'd forgotten to do something.

"Karzin?" I looked over my shoulder at him. He was reaching for the boarding house door but stopped when he heard my voice. I turned back to face him fully. “I didn’t thank you.”

“For what?” he asked.

“What do you mean?” I laughed. “You saved my life today. I would’ve died if you hadn’t been there to catch me.”

“I couldn’t let you fall.” His voice was softer, huskier than it usually was.

I was going to say something else but the thought flitted right out of my mind when I looked into his eyes.

Like a flash, I saw in my mind's eye what kissing him could be like. What being wrapped up in his strong arms and pressed against him would be like.

How those large hands of his would caress my body. How they’d pet me.

How his mouth would travel down my body, kissing it.

How his smile would look as he undressed me.

How his touch would feel between my thighs. As he gently rubbed my…

I took a jerky step back, driving the thoughts out of my mind.

“I need to take more medicine,” I stammered. “I have to get home.”

“Be safe,” Karzin nodded.

I turned around through sheer willpower. My feet did not wish to move away from this handsome alien.

Nevertheless, I had to, and I began to head for home. When I looked over my shoulder, Karzin had disappeared into the boarding house.

I bumped my hip against the door of my home to open it. The moment I did, my family descended on me like a flock of birds.

"You were due home hours ago!" my mom exclaimed. "What kept you?"

"Work was unusual today."

Cassie tore the market bags from my hands. "There's no cheese!" she exclaimed.

"The market was out. I got there near closing time," I said.

"Why were you there so late?" my mother demanded. She put her arm around my back to bring me into the house.

I winced when she put pressure on me.

"Are you hurt, Annie?" Helix asked from his spot on the floor.

"Like I said, work was unusual." I pulled one of Dr. Parr's pills from the bottle in my pack and popped it in my mouth.

"What was that? Where are you hurt? What happened?" my mother fussed.

"You were supposed to get noodles. You got rice instead," Cassie called.

"I know what I got, Cassie. If you aren't happy with it, then go to the market yourself," I snapped.

"Stop vexing your sister and tell me what happened!" my mother cried.

I carefully lowered myself to the floor beside Helix.

"You're the only sane one here," I muttered.

"I do not accept that." My father overheard what I'd said. "I'm sane as a crane."

"That wasn't a saying on Earth," I snorted.

"It still rhymes," he shrugged.

"My heart is going to give out if you keep me in suspense!" my mother insisted.

"All right!" I surrendered. I told them everything about the tremors, the crater, and Karzin. I didn't mention that something attacked us. It would only cause my mother to worry more. Instead, I said my equipment malfunctioned.

The family seemed to be more interested in Karzin than anything.

"You sent him to Finola?" my mother questioned. "She'll eat him alive."

"I think he can hold his own against her," I chuckled. I imagined Karzin and Finola staring each other down, negotiating the price of the room. I wondered who would come out on top of that negotiation. The thought of it made me smile.

The thought of Karzin turned the smile into a wistful thought.

Oh, hell.

KARZIN

The boarding housc wasn't that different from the other buildings around it. During the past few months since the Xathi were gone, many of the humans that had lost homes tried to leave behind old homes and old memories to rebuild. Several new little villages had popped up across the continent, some spread out away from other points of civilization, and others, like Somerst, were built close to some of the surviving cities.

I had never thought of how bad the humans had it. Many of them, like Annie and her family, tried to squeeze their families into homes that were barely big enough for two or three people. The fact that Annie's family had worked so hard to find a way to stay together, even at the expense of their own privacy and comfort, was admirable. Annie worked so hard to care for her family, and they relied on her to a great degree.

These people were working so hard to rebuild their lives, and I was wanting to leave them. If we hadn't opened the rift by using our experimental weapon... although the Urai were hypothesizing that the Xathi had attempted to open a rift and our use of the weapon had disrupted them...these people would never have had their lives changed so badly. We were the reason for this. It made sense that the others wanted to help fix it.

Places like the boarding house had been erected to provide temporary lodging for people looking to get out of Nyheim. From what I had seen, all of the homes were the same. They had been built from whatever materials they could find, including scrap pieces of the Xathi ship, the *Vengeance,* and anything that was salvageable from Nyheim. The nicer buildings in town had been some of the first ones built and had also made use of the sections of the *Aurora* that Fen and the Urai had deemed expendable.

This particular boarding house was a mixture of wood and metal. Actually, the main entrance to the boarding house used to be a door from the *Vengeance.* When I asked the owner, the woman named Finola, about the door, she told me that someone had offered her the door in exchange for a night's sleep. She didn't know where they had found it.

Finola was a marvel. She was an older human, and despite having lost her leg, she still worked hard trying to care for the boarding house. She knew it wasn't the most sanitary of places, and that there were some structural issues, but she also knew it was strong, and she made sure that everyone that needed a place to stay got one.

The next morning, after settling things in my room, I went back to the main room of the boarding house. General Rouhr had asked me to stay on call in case I was needed. But for the time being, I had my time to myself.

I briefly considered going back to the *Aurora*. But looking around the town, around the boarding house, something stirred in my chest.

Maybe I hadn't been there to help rebuild the human towns, or help the new settlements. But this place, this one place, I could make a difference.

"Finola," I said as I came into the main room. She turned in her wheelchair.

"Ah, Mister Karzin. What can I do for you?" she asked. She seemed to be in a good mood, something I struggled at understanding. If I had lost a leg, I knew I would struggle keeping a smile on my face.

"I was wondering if there was anything I could help

you with around here. I would hate to take up space without doing something to deserve it."

"What do you mean? You're paying for the room, that's deserving enough," she answered back.

I shrugged and sat down in a seat next to her. "Not to me. I want to help out, make myself useful to you."

"That's very nice. Thank you. If you're okay with it, I actually do have some things that need to be done."

"I am at your service, madam. Just point me in a direction and give me orders." I wasn't sure what had come over me, but the idea of helping her out made me feel better.

While I was still worried about my family and wanted desperately to find them, helping Finola was a calming substitute.

"Okay, if you insist." She wheeled her way towards the kitchen, motioning for me to follow. She pushed her way through the door and rolled over towards a small desk she had by the counter. I wondered if I would be able to convince one of the Urai to make Finola a new leg, as part of my payment to her. She grabbed something from the desk and held it out to me. It was a small card.

"What's this?"

"My ration card. It's refilled once a week and I need to use it before they run out. If I give you a list, can you get the food?"

I nodded. "Yes, ma'am. Just tell me where to go and I'll take care of it."

"Thank you. When you're done with getting the food, I'm also going to need some fresh water, if you don't mind." She looked up at me and it looked like she fully expected me to refuse.

"Which one do you want done first?" I asked.

With a small smile, she pointed to the back corner of the kitchen. I saw several water bottles there and a small cart. "If you don't mind, we're almost out of water, so if you could do that first, I'd be very grateful."

"Very well, I'll take care of it." I filled the cart with the empty water bottles, and after getting directions from Finola, took the bottles to the small well in town. I had to wait a few minutes as the people in front of me filled their bottles, or buckets, or whatever they had.

Many of them glanced at me and gave me a polite nod, but I could see that some of them were still scared to see me, or angry. I wasn't able to blame them.

When it was my turn, I filled the bottles and returned to the boarding house, where Finola had me change out the different places where the water bottles were used, then gave me the shopping list. She suggested I take the cart again, and I was glad to take her advice. I would not have been able to take her rations back just on my own.

As there was no functioning market in Somerst, I asked Fen to open a rift for me that took me to Nyheim.

"I do have other responsibilities, Strike Leader Karzin."

It was always hard to tell with the Urai if the flat tones of their voices were due to the speech pads, or annoyance. "I know, but until you teach me how to operate the rifts by myself…"

"We will see." Right now, I'd bet on annoyance.

However, she still opened the rift to Nyheim, where I secured Finola's shopping list. Of course, I purchased some extra rations and overpaid, telling the market keeper to keep the money. I knew it wasn't a lot of help, but it was something, and it made me feel better.

When I returned to the boarding house, I put the food away where Finola told me to and volunteered to help her with some cleaning and general maintenance on the place. She didn't hold back. I cleaned several of the rooms, helped her with a repair job to the back door and in the kitchen, and did a little bit of yard work.

She had started a garden but was struggling with getting it going. It was hard for her to work the garden in her wheelchair. She had to get herself out of the chair and crawl through the garden. I was more determined than ever to get her a new leg so she could be more mobile.

It had turned into a long day. After the repairs in the kitchen and the garden work, I had volunteered to get the supplies she needed to patch up her roof, then went up there myself to do the work. It felt good. I hadn't worked that hard in a long time, and to see Finola's face at the end of the day when I was finished made everything worth it.

After I cleaned myself up a bit, I joined Finola in the common room "So," I asked, "what do you want me to cook tonight for dinner?"

"Oh, that's okay. I'm usually the one that gets dinner taken care of," she answered back.

"I understand, but I wouldn't mind helping out. I find that I actually like the work, keeps my mind off of other things," I said with a sad smile.

She put her hand on my arm and gave it a gentle squeeze. "Sometimes, it's hard for us to remember that you and your friends had your own suffering by the Xathi before here. Did you lose someone?"

I nodded. "I'm still looking for some way to contact my home."

"I'm assuming that means you haven't yet, have you?"

I shook my head.

She patted my arm. "I'm sorry. Let's change the subject back to dinner. I'm not used to people helping much, but I'd really appreciate it if you really do want to help."

"I can't think of anything better," I said to her with a smile. We spent the next hour preparing a very tasty stew, then ate it together in the common area. It was only the two of us, so we talked. Very few subjects were off-limits.

"So where were you living till now?" she asked me.

"I was living on the *Aurora,*" I replied. "But the general has asked me to stay close."

"That's the alien ship?"

I nodded.

"With all the soldiers dispersed, it must have been lonely," she stated.

"I've not given up on searching for a way home. And I refuse to give up. My crewmates may have all given up and decided to cast their lot on this planet, but I refuse to forget my family and my people."

"I can understand that."

I stared at her. "You can?"

"I think you need to get over your crew. Sure, they're probably trying to make the best of their bad situation, but if you think you need to do something, then you need to do it. The rest of the people be damned. They're just being spoilsports because you're not following them."

I had to agree with her, they were trying to make the best of a bad situation. I just didn't want to see it.

"Do you mind if I ask..."

She shrugged. "How I lost my leg? It's probably not that interesting of a story to a soldier."

I'd like to hear it, anyhow."

She sighed and looked off in the distance. "When the Xathi first attacked Fraga, I fought. We all did. Eventually, they bombed our building, and I fell down an open sewer grate. The waters of the sewer just contaminated my wound. I was too weak to get out, not injured enough not to know what was happening."

"That's terrible."

"I nearly died. When people finally found me, my leg had already begun to rot. They had to cut it off in order to save my life."

I felt horrible for her.

"Don't you worry about me. I'm a tough old bird. I'll survive," she said.

I smiled. "I'm sure you will."

After we said goodnight to one another, I put in a call to Fen to see about a leg for Finola. After that, I crawled into bed to sleep, happy with my potential surprise.

Early in the morning, a message came in from Rouhr.

There were several holes that had appeared suddenly in Duvest, and no one could give too many details. I was to take Annie there in the morning to investigate.

It was going to be a long day.

But somehow, the thought I'd be spending it with Annie made it slightly more bearable.

Slightly.

ANNIE

The next morning, it wasn't Cassie's rolling or Helix's sleep talk, but a knock on the door that roused me from sleep.

"What the fuck?" Cassie grumbled.

"Language," I scolded her as I sat up from my sleeping mat. My back hardly hurt and was only a little stiff. Whatever Dr. Parr had given me had done the trick.

"Who's knocking at this hour?" my mother called from her room.

"Someone with a death wish," Cassie replied.

"Thanks for getting the door, Cass," I said loud enough for my parents to hear.

Cassie shot me a glare then climbed up from her mat. She stomped across the room as if trying to be as disruptive as possible. She used to be so sweet. I spoiled her when she was a baby. I tried to keep my annoyance with her under control. She'd been through a lot and she didn't know how to cope. She'd figure it out eventually.

"The jolly green giant is at the door," she called over her shoulder.

"What?" I jumped up and wrapped my blanket around myself. I only wore a tank top and shorts underneath. Cassie opened the door wider to reveal Karzin standing on our doorstep.

"Sorry to wake you," Karzin said, looking at Cass out of the corner of his eye. His voice didn't contain a trace of genuine apology. At that moment, he noticed the inside of the house and how small and simple it was. He hid the look of shock that came over his expression, but not before I noticed it. "Annie, something's happened. General Rouhr is asking for us."

"General Rouhr?" My mother stepped out of her room, tying her robe over her nightgown. She gasped at the sight of Karzin in the doorway. His shoulders were wider than the door. "The alien who killed all the Xathi?"

"He commands the aliens that killed the Xathi," Karzin corrected, with a slight smile.

"What does he want with you?" My mother turned her attention from Karzin to me.

"Is it something to do with the crater?" I asked Karzin.

"He didn't say." Karzin was still looking around the small room. I tried not to let myself feel embarrassed. There was nothing wrong with where we lived. Lots of people had it worse.

"Let me get dressed. Wait outside," I ordered before I ducked into the bathroom. I realized too late that I must've sounded rude, barking orders at him like that.

I quickly showered. The water was ice cold. I wouldn't have time to go to the well this morning. Dad would have to go.

Within five minutes, I showered, dried my hair and tugged on clean clothes. I told my father about the water as I dashed out the door.

"What about breakfast?" Cassie called after me.

"Learn to cook!" I called back.

"You sleep in that front room?" Karzin asked as I followed him to the shuttle depot. I nodded. I really didn't want to talk about my living situation with him.

"Where are we going?" I asked, effectively changing the subject.

"Duvest," Karzin replied.

"This shuttle only goes to Nyheim. We'll have to catch another one from there," I explained.

"There isn't a faster way?" Karzin asked.

"Not unless you have your own transport unit," I replied. Karzin looked at me with a sly grin on his face.

"I have something better."

He pulled a device out of his pocket and spoke into it.

"You there, Fen?" he asked.

"What do you want?" A computerized voice replied.

"If I send you my location, can you open a rift to get me to Duvest?" he asked.

"Fine," the voice replied.

"What's a rift?" I asked.

"It's what our ship and the Xathi ship fell through," Karzin explained.

"Why are you opening one?" I stared up at him, wide-eyed.

"Some time ago, some of my associates found an orb that can control rifts on a small scale. We've used it hundreds of times to transport refugees. It's perfectly safe," Karzin assured me. A few feet in front of us, a vertical band of light appeared out of thin air. It widened until I could see an entirely different landscape on the other side. Several townspeople stopped to stare at the rift.

"After you," Karzin gestured.

Without knowing what we were doing, I felt my hand reach for his. He wrapped his large hand around mine and I held on tight to his.

I held my breath as I stepped up to the rift as if I was about to dive into a pool of water. I took one step through. It was like my body was trapped in ice. For a moment, I didn't think I'd be able to move but then my foot came into contact with the ground on the other side of the rift. Just like that, I was through.

Karzin followed right behind me and asked Fen, whatever that was, to close the rift behind him. It flickered away like it was never there.

"I did not like that," I shivered. Karzin opened his mouth, then thought better of it.

"I was going to say you get used to it but I still haven't," he chuckled. "You did well for your first time. I thought you would get stuck."

"What happens if you get stuck?" I asked.

"I don't know," Karzin shrugged.

"You're not reassuring," I grumbled.

"Do you think we could release our hands now?" Karzin asked, and I could see a faint smile.

I hastily dropped my grip and pulled my hand away. I blushed a bit and looked down at the ground.

I was just about to say something when we were interrupted.

"Hey!" A man ran up to us, looking frantic and bleeding from one dirt-covered arm. "You're one of those aliens, right? You're here to help us?"

"We were told of an incident," Karzin replied. "What's happened?"

We followed the man farther into the city. I noticed immediately that everything was far too quiet. There were none of the usual sounds associated with a bustling city.

"I don't know," the man said. "I think we were attacked. Have the Xathi returned?"

"No," Karzin assured him. "General Rouhr and his team have been carefully monitoring the planet for Xathi survivors. There are none."

"Then what did this?" The man brought us to one of the main city squares of Duvest. It looked like a bomb had gone off. Windows were shattered and glass covered the cobblestone square. The fountain in the center of the square, which looked like it had been out of operation for some time, was cracked and broken. People were strewn across the square in various states of distress.

There was no sign of what caused such damage, except for about half a dozen perfectly circular craters dispersed throughout the square.

Unlike the crater we'd explored yesterday, the holes weren't very deep, just enough that if anyone had fallen in, they'd likely die from the impact.

"Karzin." I put my hand on his shoulder to get his attention then pointed to the craters. "Those look like miniature versions of the one we found out in the desert."

"Are you comfortable with investigating alone while I help these people?" Karzin asked.

"The craters aren't going anywhere. Let's help the people first," I replied. He gave me a brief smile before turning his attention back to the man.

"How many injured?" he asked.

"At least twenty. Four are dead," the man explained.

"Are there doctors in the town?" Karzin asked.

"Yes, they've already been called," the man replied.

"You're hurt, as well," Karzin noticed, "yet you don't know what happened?"

"I can't remember," the man said.

"What's your name?"

"Mac."

"Okay, Mac," Karzin sighed. "Did you hit your head at any point?"

"I don't think so," Mac said. "I feel no pain in my head. Just my arm." He held out his arm for Karzin to examine. I peered around Karzin to have a look for myself.

"Looks like this was done by a shard of glass," Karzin said. "Go clean it, then see a doctor for stitches." The man nodded and stumbled away.

"How does he not remember anything?" I wondered

"Shock does things to the brain," Karzin shrugged.

We stepped around the body of an elderly man to reach a young woman, sobbing and cowering against a wall.

"Let me," I urged Karzin. "I'm less intimidating."

"Fair enough," Karzin agreed.

I knelt down beside the woman, whose pale hair was stained with blood.

"Are you all right?" As soon as the words were out of my mouth, I sighed to myself. Stupid question.

"What happened to me?" She looked up at me, her pale blue eyes brimming with tears.

"That's what we were hoping you could tell us," I said. "We're here to help, but we can't do that if we don't know what happened."

"I don't know," she sobbed. "I was walking to my Nan's house one minute, the next, I'm covered in blood and there were broken buildings on the street."

"You remember nothing?" I asked. She shook her head, hiding her face behind her hands. "That's okay. Doctors are on their way. Stay here and don't move too much. You're going to be okay." I stood and walked back over to Karzin.

"She doesn't remember anything," I told him. We made our way around the square, asking everyone who could speak what had happened. No one seemed to have any idea. Everyone was going about their usual business, then suddenly found themselves injured and the square destroyed.

"Are you sure it's not the Xathi?" I whispered so I wouldn't cause unnecessary panic. "They were able to mess with people's minds."

"If it was Xathi, General Rouhr would've known already," Karzin replied. "Besides, the Xathi specialize in indoctrination, not memory wiping. Still, I'll call Dr. Parr down here. On the off chance it is Xathi, she'll be able to tell if any of these people are at risk of hybridism."

"While you do that, I'm going to look at the craters," I said. "From the sound of it, the ground is going to be the only thing that can give us any information."

I'd only grabbed my usual bag when I left the house in a rush. Thankfully, I always carried some field equipment with me. I counted seven craters total. I had only six sample vials. I picked the six craters that were closest to an injured person and scooped a small sample from each into a vial.

Nothing stood out to me immediately. The dirt looked as one would expect it to look. I was anxious to get back to my lab. I hadn't yet gotten a chance to test the samples from yesterday.

"The doctors are arriving," Karzin told me. "There's nothing more we can do here."

"I need to get to Nyheim and test these," I held up my sample vials. "I'd rather not go through another rift to get there."

"Fine, we'll take the boring public shuttle," Karzin agreed nonchalantly as if I couldn't see the troubled look in his eyes.

I nodded my head. I'd rather take the unreliable and overcrowded shuttles any day than go through another one of those things.

How little I knew of what was to come.

KARZIN

"We need to get back to Nyheim and talk to General Rouhr," I had told Annie. "He needs to know what happened here."

We got our gear together, loaded up into the shuttle, and went back to Nyheim. What we had seen in Duvest had been disconcerting, to say the least.

The fact that the attack had happened in the center of a busy city square was scary enough. It was the idea that no one remembered anything about it that worried me more.

We flew in silence back to Nyheim. Annie looked at her samples and the information she had gathered, while I sat and tried to figure out the attack. If it had been the same entity that had created the crater near the *Aurora*, then we were going to have problems.

I actually found it just as worrisome that whatever this was could make numerous circles in civilized areas than a large circle in the wilderness. While the giant crater was terrifying to think about, a collection of smaller holes in a concentrated area had me wracking my brain to find solutions, defenses, and ways to deal with it.

We landed, gathered our gear, and planned to head to the general's office, but he met us at the airfield instead.

"I didn't want to wait. Tell me what's going on in Duvest."

A human official hurried us into a small room, while I began the report I'd mentally prepared on the trip back. "Well, sir, there are seven holes in the city square. Perfect circles, just like the one near the *Aurora*."

"How many dead and injured?"

"We don't know for sure but early indications indicate four fatalities and over a dozen injured. There isn't an exact count at the moment, though. No one remembers how anything happened, sir. For some reason, people's memories seemed to be affected."

"Well, skrell." He paced away and back several times, processing the information. When he finally came back and stopped, he looked at Annie. "What about you, young lady? What information do you have for me?"

"Not much to give you, General. I can tell you, the

craters hold the same shape, and the initial deposits that I collected look the same, but I won't know until I get into my lab." She looked up at him, then apologized. "I'm sorry."

He did a double-take. "Why are you apologizing?"

"Because I don't have any better information for you, sir. I wish I did."

"I know you do. I'm not upset with you in any way," he said calmly. "You have a job to do, and I need you to do it. I'm just upset this is happening and we don't have a remedy for it yet. This is where you come in."

"Yes, sir," she said with a nod.

Rouhr looked at me, then back at Annie. "Do what you can. I expect results as soon as you can get them." With that, he walked away, and he was not happy.

"Did we do something wrong?" Annie asked.

I looked at her and shook my head. "No. He just takes on too much responsibility and feels that everything is on him. He's worried. He came very close to making himself sick over the Xathi, so he's probably wondering if this is somehow our fault."

"Why does he think this is your guys' fault?"

"Because we brought the Xathi here, and he most likely thinks that it set off a chain of events that will end up with more people hurt." I picked up our gear. "Let's get to your lab."

We walked to the airfield exit and got into a small

vehicle to drive to her lab. With her directions, we arrived within a few minutes and took everything inside. She seemed to be proud of her little lab and showed me around a bit before we went into her own corner. I held back my smile as she showed me what things were and explained it all to me.

Watching her happily bustle around made something warm in my chest, just for a moment. "Do you think you'll be able to decipher your samples?"

She gave me a look that essentially said I was stupid. "Decipher? You don't decipher things in this lab. You discover, you learn, you…you…you dissect and dismantle until you get down to the basest materials and you take that information to learn about the beginnings of everything."

Now it was my turn to look at her awkwardly. "You can learn about the beginnings from dirt?"

"Without a doubt. If you dig down deep enough, you can find the beginnings of life in an area, or on a planet. People think geology is simply looking at rocks, but it's so much more than that! It may not be as fancy as some of the other sciences, but you can learn a tremendous amount that the others can't." She was beaming with pride and I couldn't help but laugh.

She set about running her samples through the machines that she had.

I watched her work as I sat at the far end of the lab.

She was tiny. Not a warrior. But still, utterly fascinating. Her lithe body moved from station to station, intent on her tasks. Her brow furrowed, small white teeth absently nibbling on her lush pink lower lip.

My gaze was riveted to her mouth, the urge to taste her almost overpowering. I wanted to go over and wrap my arms around her. To lift her up and feel her body rub against mine. My blood began to simmer with the lust that Valorni were known for. Her figure and attitude brought about the feelings that I had long told myself as a warrior I would never experience.

And despite all my heated stares, she worked. It didn't take long for me to sense that something was wrong. I walked over to her to see.

"What is it?"

She shook her head, ran her hand through her hair, and blew out a large breath of air through her lips. "I'm not finding anything. My equipment just isn't capable of figuring out the makeup and composition of some of the samples. These," she pointed to roughly two-thirds of her samples, "my machines can test and give me information, and none of it is what Rouhr is wanting. It's fantastic for me and my scientific pursuits, but it means nothing to what's happening in Duvest."

Then she pointed at the remaining samples. "On

these, though, my machines can't give me any information at all. Everything comes up as an error."

She was stressed, I could see that. She was struggling to figure things out and it was frustrating her so much. This wasn't something I could fight, something I could fix. But surely there was something I could do. Then a small light of brilliance popped into my mind.

"Give me a moment," I said to her as I walked out of the lab. I got onto my comm to talk to Fen.

"Fen. Would you care to open a rift for me?"

"What is your current location, friend Karzin?"

"At the moment, I am with a human scientist in Nyheim. We need to borrow the *Aurora's* science facility, if you don't mind," I said over the comm.

"Why would this human scientist require our laboratories?"

I explained the situation to her, including how the systems that Annie was using weren't able to decipher what the samples were.

I was unable to tell if Fen was frustrated with me or not when she answered. "Very well. I shall open a rift in three of your minutes. Do not be late."

I rushed back to Annie. "Want to use a more sophisticated lab and better equipment?"

"Of course! But where?" Her eyes were wide with wonder.

"Good. Pack up, our transportation will be ready in about two minutes, and we need to be outside when it is." We hurried as we grabbed everything, then rushed outside.

"No," she whined. "Not again!"

Too bad for her, I didn't give her a chance. I turned and dragged her through the rift, her yelps echoing behind me.

As we stepped out of the rift and back onto solid ground, Annie ripped her hand out of mine and dropped to her knees. "Ohh," she stuttered. "Why is it always so fucking cold?"

"Try doing it several times a day," I said to her.

She looked at me.

I nodded, a small grin on my face.

"You people are nuts!" She got to her feet and I turned her around to see the remnants of the *Aurora*. "Oh. My. God."

I led her inside and we were met at the laboratory doors by Fen. Annie had never seen an Urai and she had lost all ability to speak coherently, leaving me to explain in my simple ways what had happened and what we needed.

"Very well. Our equipment is ready for your use, Doctor Parker. I will assist you," Fen said as she opened the doors to let us in. If seeing another alien species that made the rest of us look like brutish beasts wasn't enough to completely destroy her mind, the Urai science facility was. I don't believe I had ever seen anyone so excited, or so at a loss for words.

The noises that came from Annie were both unnerving and hilarious. I had never thought that sounds like that could possibly come from a human, but Annie was giving little yelps, yips, giggles, and some sort of squeal that I didn't think was possible from anything living.

After a few short moments of Annie losing her mind, she finally looked at Fen and me and gave the world's biggest, happiest smile, then settled down into coherence with an undertone of joy. "I'm sorry. I've just never seen anything this fantastic before."

"I believe you have soil samples that need to be analyzed," Fen said calmly.

Annie cleared her throat and settled down even more. "Uh, yes. Yes, we do." For the next several hours, Annie and Fen analyzed and studied all of the samples, and Annie was beyond excited by the information that the Urai equipment was able to give her.

There was one minor problem, however.

"I must apologize, Doctor Parker. Not even our systems are capable of deciphering the samples that you have brought, not completely," Fen announced.

"It's okay, Fen. While we haven't discovered what it

is, we have discovered that it is an organic material," Annie said.

"What does that mean?" I asked.

Both women looked at me. "It means that whatever caused the craters is alive. It's a living thing," Annie answered.

If it was a living thing, we'd be able to fight it, stop it, right?

But what could make those holes? And why couldn't we remember?

ANNIE

The results from the *Aurora's* superior lab caused me deep concern. The *Aurora's* lab outstripped mine in every way imaginable and it still couldn't tell me what had created those craters.

I couldn't shake the feeling that I'd made a mistake at some point. After all, I didn't have enough supplies with me to collect full samples. I was unfamiliar with much of the equipment. This was my first time taking on such a project. The unusual results had me wondering if I was fit for it.

But Fen had been right there, working alongside me. And she'd reached the same results.

After pacing the lab for the better part of an hour, I decided to go find Karzin. If anything, he'd be able to point me in the right direction.

I found him in the corridor, walking toward the lab.

"I was just coming to see you," he informed me. "You've been in there a while now."

"Worried about me?" I teased.

"Humans turn stupid when they don't eat enough. I was only coming to make sure you hadn't been affected," he explained with a raised eyebrow.

"I'm not stupid, but I'm stumped." I folded my arms across my chest. "I need a second opinion on the samples. I need fresh eyes."

"I might be able to help you with that," Karzin rubbed his jaw, eyes distant.

"That is why I came to you. You always have a solution tucked up your sleeve." I gave him a friendly clap on the arm.

"Don't thank me yet. I've…what's the human expression? Bombed bridges?"

"I think you mean burned bridges," I corrected.

Karzin nodded as he pulled his communication device out of his pocket. He made some adjustments before speaking into it.

"Axtin, you there?" There was a long pause, punctuated by rustling sounds.

"You have a lot of nerve calling me up," a gruff voice replied.

"I've always had a lot of nerve," Karzin replied.

"Is that why you hide on the *Aurora* instead of facing us at meetings?" the voice growled.

"I see you're out of the loop, Axtin," Karzin drawled, trying to sound unbothered. I watched him work the muscles in his jaw. "I'm on a mission."

"Skrell," Axtin scoffed. "Like General Rouhr would give you an assignment after the way you've turned your back on us."

I felt guilty for overhearing Axtin's words. This was personal, private. I made a move to step back, but Karzin stopped me with a reassuring smile.

"Did you hear about the incident at Duvest this morning?" he asked into the comm.

"What incident?" Axtin snapped.

"That's what I thought," Karzin smirked. "Anyway, I didn't call to talk to you. I need Leena."

"What do you want with her?" Axtin demanded.

"I'm working with a human geologist named Andromeda Parker-"

"Annie!" I snapped before I could stop myself.

Mischief glinted in Karzin's eyes. "Annie Parker. She collected samples from the incident. We brought them to the *Aurora* for analysis, however there's still a lot we don't know. I'd like Leena to come give her expert opinion," Karzin explained.

"Leena wants nothing to do with you, either," Axtin replied.

"Excuse me?" A woman's voice spoke from the background. "Did you just refuse a job on my behalf?"

"Hello, Leena," Karzin called through the comm. "Go easy on Axtin. He's just pouting."

"Axtin has every right to not want to talk to you after everything you've done," Leena chided. "However, I'd be happy to look over the geologist's samples tomorrow."

"Thank you, Leena. Buy a shorter leash for Axtin while you're at it," Karzin said.

"Don't push it," Leena warned before disconnecting the call.

"She'll be here tomorrow," Karzin grinned.

"Great." I wasn't sure how to process everything I'd just heard. Clearly, there were some unaddressed issues between Karzin and the rest of his team. I decided not to press it. It wasn't my business.

"You should stay here for the night," Karzin said suddenly.

"What?"

"Leena is coming tomorrow. It doesn't seem worth it for you to go all the way home just to come back, especially since you don't like traveling by rift," Karzin explained.

He was right. I hated the rifts. If I never had to travel by rift again, that would be perfectly fine with me.

"But, where..." I looked around, wondering how

many of the rooms were set up for a human. Did it matter?

Or was he thinking…

"Plenty of cabins still ready for occupation." Thankfully, Karzin didn't seem to notice my heated cheeks, just waited for my answer.

The idea was logical and the *Aurora* looked like a comfortable place to sleep. Just once, it might be nice to sleep on a proper bed in my own room, like I had before the Xathi invasion.

As long as I could keep my imagination to myself.

"All right," I agreed with a smile. "I'll need to let my family know somehow."

"You can talk to them on this." Karzin held up his communication device.

"Will it work with older human comm units?" I asked.

"Only one way to find out." Karzin tossed the device toward me. I barely managed to catch it. After looking at it for a few moments, I knew I wouldn't be able to use it.

"I can't read your language," I told him.

"I'll make the call, then," Karzin offered.

"Mom will be surprised to hear from a Valorni," I laughed.

"If she's as resilient as you are, she'll be fine," Karzin chuckled.

"She's tougher," I replied.

"So, you're the runt of the family, then?" Karzin asked.

"I wouldn't say that." I made a show of being offended before bursting into laughter. I gave Karzin the information to contact my family.

After a few moments, my mother answered. The connection was faint and filled with static interference. Apparently alien to human technology didn't integrate well, after all.

"Hello?" I heard my mother's voice.

"Mom! It's Annie." I spoke louder than I normally would.

"Andromeda? Where are you?" she demanded.

"I'm working overnight," I explained.

"How come you don't get mad at *her* for calling you Andromeda?" Karzin demanded.

"Shush!" I urged him.

"Who was that?" my mother asked.

"Karzin, the Valorni that came to the door this morning. I'm staying overnight at work. Don't expect me home! Love you!" I hung up quickly to avoid answering a million questions. "It's like I'm thirteen again," I laughed.

"Is that a significant age for humans?" Karzin asked.

"Kind of," I shrugged. "Is there a place to eat here? I haven't had a bite all day."

"There is," Karzin grinned. He jerked his head for me to follow him. "We used to have the best cook in the known universe but Snipes left to cook for a refugee kitchen. I always knew that old alien was soft-hearted."

Karzin took me to a cafeteria of sorts that was mostly empty, except for a few Urai.

"The new cook is good but not as good as old Snipes," Karzin sighed wistfully. I laughed at his melodrama. Looking at the food that was offered, I recognized much of it.

"I haven't had some of this stuff in months," I sighed as I piled my plate high with foods that were once common but now could be considered delicacies.

Karzin and I sat at a table in the corner of the hall and ate in companionable silence. After I cleaned my plate, I went back for second servings.

"If you were hungry, you should've let me know sooner," Karzin exclaimed.

"It's not that," I explained. "At home, I get the tiniest portions. I want to eat as much as I can while I don't have to share."

"That doesn't seem fair," Karzin frowned.

"I can always get a bite to eat in the city," I shrugged. "They rarely leave Somerst."

"You're the sole provider for your family?" Karzin asked. I nodded between bites.

"Until desk jobs are more common again, Helix

won't be able to work. My mom is a ball of nervous energy. She's scared of everything now, not that I blame her. Dad spends all of his time helping out around the town, but he rarely makes money off it," I explained.

"And your sister?" Karzin asked.

"Cass is," I struggled to come up with the right words. "She's not used to the shock of losing everything. She doesn't know how to process it. If she did manage to get a job, I don't think she'd last long."

"So it's all on your shoulders," Karzin nodded.

"I have a job I love that's just gotten interesting," I grinned. "I don't have any complaints."

"That's very admirable of you," Karzin smiled. We ate in silence for a few more moments, but eventually, my curiosity got the better of me. I had to know why things with this Axtin character were so tense.

"What sort of alien is Axtin?" I asked.

"He's a Valorni, as well," Karzin replied.

"He didn't seem happy to hear from you," I ventured, keeping my eyes on my plate.

"There's some tension," Karzin admitted. "Valorni don't tend to hide their emotions." I waited for Karzin to offer more information, but he didn't.

"What happened?" I asked.

"It's a long story." Karzin gave me a soft smile. "Not one I'm in the mood to tell tonight."

"That's okay," I tried to give him a reassuring smile.

"You can talk to me about it if you ever want to. You saved my life, so I'm not allowed to judge you."

My words made Karzin chuckle. "That's right. I get to hold that over your head for the rest of your life," he replied.

"You can hold that over me, or you can make fun of my name. You have to pick one," I teased, finishing my dinner, finally full.

"That's no way to talk to the Valorni who saved your life, Andromeda," Karzin shot back. I flicked a piece of food at him. It landed on his shirt.

"How can someone so handsome be such a pain in the ass?" I sighed.

"You think I'm handsome?" Karzin blinked.

"You're not awful to look at," I shrugged. "You're still a pain in the ass, though."

"I could say the same about you," Karzin replied.

"I'm not handsome," I rolled my eyes, taking another sip of my drink.

"No, you're beautiful." My hand stilled halfway to my mouth as Karzin's words sunk in. Before I could stammer or brush him off, he leaned across the table and pressed his lips against mine.

His lips were warm and solid.

I dropped my fork, not caring if food splattered everywhere, and placed a hand on his cheek.

I felt the world melt away as he continued to kiss

me. The power and magnetism of this exquisite alien with the body of a god made me forget everything.

For a moment, nothing else mattered. No one else existed. His tongue danced with mine and I gave up even trying to remember my name, let alone any responsibilities.

All I felt was him.

All I was…was for him.

He pulled away too soon, leaving me wanting more. I looked at him, slightly breathless and dazed. My voice was light and breathy when I next spoke.

"Like I said, pain in the ass."

KARZIN

The kiss had been a welcome change to everything in my life.

It felt good.

She felt good.

Which brought about my dilemma.

I wanted to help Annie, and the people here. They had suffered much because of our war, and now they were being attacked by something else that could very well have been our fault. Annie was working hard to figure out what was the cause of the craters.

I knew that she wasn't the only one looking into it, but it seemed as though her perspective was the one that would find the answers. Somehow, it felt as though Annie would be the one to solve this.

It was Annie, with the help of Fen and the Urai

laboratory, that had discovered that some of the sediments were organic, and that meant that whatever was causing the craters and seismic activity was a living, breathing being. In the few short days since I had first met her, she had come to impress me more than the other human women had. They all worked hard at what they did, and they'd all proved vital in our fight against the Xathi, but they just always seemed to be trying too hard, or too stubborn, or just too annoying for my tastes.

Annie had, when we first met, stood up for herself and shown me that she was more than willing to do what was necessary. To be completely truthful, the moment she had snapped at me on our first shuttle ride was the moment I knew I had judged her wrongly. It was that moment that made me decide to give her a chance to be something more than just another ungrateful, annoying human.

When she took me to Somerst, I was shocked to see how she and many other humans were forced to live. At first, seeing the boarding house she recommended, I had thought that I would rather sleep in the open than there, but her judgment and opinion of Finola had persuaded me to give it a chance.

Now, Fen was working on a leg for Finola so she could have better mobility, and I enjoyed working with her.

Then, when I knocked on Annie's door and saw her and her family's living arrangements, I was speechless. I saw the embarrassment in her eyes, but she shouldn't have been.

The sacrifice they had all made, and the work that she put in to care for them…it was all admirable. She was doing everything she could for her family.

And I wasn't.

I was sitting on this planet, enjoying the company of a lovely woman, while my family and my people were spending every second of their lives fighting for another second.

The only imaginable alternative to their fighting was too much to accept.

Thoughts spinning, I gave up on sleep, returned to the control room, and brought up the satellite reports. They were as expected, empty, but I refused to accept that.

I just needed to find the right spot was all.

The *Aurora* was a spectacular ship, or at least had been. The rooms could be sound-proofed with the push of a button, and before all of this happened, I had spent many a night forcing the Urai to use their soundproofing. I had launched many probes, sixteen, and nearly a dozen satellites into space to try to widen the net of visibility.

When Fen and Rouhr questioned me about the

number of objects I launched, I told them it was a double benefit. While they were looking for a way back home, they would also be monitoring space to see if anything was coming here.

That was how I'd gotten away with it. Now, with Fen, most likely Pem, and Annie the only ones here thanks to the evacuation, I decided to launch another satellite. There was a section of space that didn't have the coverage I wanted.

As the control center shook a bit from the launch, I manipulated the satellite scanners and modulated their frequencies. Maybe we were just monitoring on the wrong wavelength.

The night passed slowly, and as per almost every other night since the Xathi were destroyed, I found nothing. What in the skrell was I doing wrong? Why couldn't I find anything? Was I really that useless that I couldn't even find my way home?

Something set off a sensor on one of the farthest satellites. My heart raced as I checked on it. It was a simple asteroid, barely larger than an escape pod. I let out a yell of frustration and threw my chair across the command center. "Aarrhhhh!" I screamed. "Why can't I make this work?" As my words echoed around the room, I stood and stared at the now broken chair. It had done nothing wrong, it had actually done everything right.

I was the one that was wrong. I rubbed my eyes, ran my hands through my hair, and cursed myself for being an idiot.

After cleaning up and repairing the chair, I did something I hadn't wanted to do.

I grabbed my comm unit and called up Dax. I wasn't sure why, but I needed someone to talk to and he was the most mellow member of any of the strike teams. Regardless of his disappointment in me, I knew he would at least talk to me.

His voice came over the comm, and as usual, he expressed concern for a person's well-being before anything else. "You're calling unusually late, Karzin. Is there anything wrong?"

"No, no, Daxion. I am sorry to be calling you this late in the night," I answered back. "I…I was looking for some advice."

"I am glad to hear that nothing is wrong, my friend "

I didn't really want to talk to him, but I was near the end of my wits and everything I tried failed. So, "I… forgive me for being blunt, cousin, but I wanted to know how you could be happy here. Our people are dying, yet you've managed to find happiness. How?" I knew my voice made my words sound accusatory, and that wasn't my intention, but I knew of no other way to ask.

I could hear him breathe over the comm as he

hesitated to answer. "I...I am unsure how to answer that without upsetting you, cousin."

"Just tell me."

"As you wish. I have not forgotten about our people, none of us have. What we *have* done, is we've talked to one another. Axtin and I speak to one another almost daily about anything and everything that enters our minds. As a matter of fact, we were speaking just now when you contacted us."

Axtin's voice came on next. "Dax is right. We talk, not just about what is happening here on Ankou, but also in our lives and about back home. It doesn't solve anything, but it helps."

I was surprised to hear civility and care in Axtin's voice, considering the last time we spoke the tension had been almost too thick to breathe. "But, how can you just sit here and laugh and smile while our people are dying?"

I heard both of them take in a deep breath. My words had been blunt, but they had been said. It was Axtin that answered first. "I worry about my friends and family every day. I truly do. I know it probably doesn't seem that way, but I do. I, for me anyway, I have to continue to be me and continue to push and fight or I'll lose my mind. The way I look at it is, if I change who I am due to grief, then I'm letting our people down."

Dax's voice came on next. "It also helps that Axtin

has found Leena, and that I have found Amira. They also speak to us daily and try to help us through. The humans have a bit of an understanding of our pain."

"I know that," I said. "But…" I looked around the room, searching for words. The other two stayed silent while I thought. "But how do you not lose your minds with not knowing about our homes?"

"That's the thing," Daxion answered. "It's different for us all. Axtin works with, and trains, the human soldiers. I work closely with Amira, trying to learn from her. I know that Tu'ver and Rouhr put their concentration on the rebuilding, while Vrehx is occupied with Jeneva's pregnancy and her attempts to domesticate some of the life on the planet to help replenish food stuffs. We all had to find something different to occupy our minds."

Axtin cut in. "I think about the good things. We're still alive. We got lucky and destroyed the Xathi that came here, made some good friends, we're living on a crazy planet with insane things, and some of us have found families of our own. You know my story. The fact that Leena and I are together has made me happier than I've ever been. She's *the* good thing in my life. I try to focus on that."

We spoke a little longer before I ended the comm. Each of them had found something in their lives to occupy their minds.

What did I have?

The first thought that came to mind was Annie and how I had come to enjoy her company. She had led me to Finola, and it felt good to help Finola and to make her life a little easier. But the harder I tried to think of positives, the less I could think of anything at all.

I wanted to help Annie, I really did. What she was doing was important, but what I was doing was important, as well. Our people needed help and I couldn't help them. If I helped Annie, then I wasn't searching, but if I searched, I wasn't helping Annie.

What was I to do?

I stared at the computer consoles, lost as to what the right choice was.

ANNIE

When I woke up the next morning, the first thought that entered my mind was about kissing Karzin and how I wouldn't mind doing it again.

I hadn't expected him to kiss me, right there at the table. If I'd known it was coming, hopefully I would've acted differently. Immediately calling him a pain in the ass afterward wasn't my smoothest move.

At least he'd thought it was funny.

I climbed out of bed and checked the time. Leena would be arriving within the hour. I needed to prepare, even though I wanted nothing more than to lie in that plush bed all day.

I took a shower, savoring the scalding hot water. It felt good. Sensations of pleasure ran through me as I closed my eyes and let my mind wander.

What would it be like to have Karzin in the shower with me? To use his deft fingers and large hands to soap my body down?

I wondered if his stripes went all the way around his body.

I imagined myself licking those stripes with my tongue. Bringing the large warrior to his knees with my hands and my mouth. Conquering him.

And then letting him conquer me.

My skin was as red as a beet when I finished. I didn't have extra clothes, so I tugged on what I wore yesterday. Thankfully, they weren't too wrinkled or too dirty. I didn't want Leena to think I was a slob.

I had a few minutes to spare, so I thought I'd try to find Karzin. I went to the cafeteria where we ate the night before but he wasn't there. The Urai cook from last night was there preparing breakfast. I grabbed a cup of coffee and a plate of proper eggs and toast.

"Have you seen the big Valorni I was here with last night?" I asked. He simply shook his head. Fen had a touchpad that enabled her to speak to us but I don't think this cook had one. At that moment, I realized how strange it was for a Urai, who did not possess a mouth, to be given the job of cook. Even more baffling, he was fantastic at it. How did he know that his creations tasted right? I wanted to ask but I didn't want to be rude.

I ate quickly before continuing my search for Karzin. I didn't know the layout of the *Aurora* at all. I didn't know the first place to look for him. In the end, I decided to walk toward the lab and hope I saw him on the way there.

I didn't.

Ignoring the twinge in my gut, I paused at the door, glancing down the corridor one more time. What had I expected? I'd known from the beginning that he had his own, very different priorities.

When I entered the lab, a woman was already there. She was petite, with severe features and pale blonde hair.

"Are you Leena?" I asked.

"I am." She stuck out her hand for me to shake. She had an iron grip and gave such a thorough handshake that I nearly spilled my coffee.

"Am I late?" I asked.

"No, I'm always early. Plus, I wanted to see the old lab. I miss this place. It's much better than the one I'm currently using." She looked around the pristine room with a fond smile.

"That's exactly what I said when I got here," I grinned.

"I'm hoping we'll be able to fully integrate Urai tech into our cities one day, but that's a long way off," Leena mused. Everything she said sounded so clever and professional, I felt like a moron, an out-of-place moron. I wondered if she knew this was my first real assignment.

"The samples and analysis results are here if you want to take a look," I cleared my throat and tried to sound like I'd done this a thousand times.

"Perfect." Leena stepped over to the counter I worked at yesterday. I pulled up the data on the console and stepped back to let her work.

"How unusual," she murmured.

"Neither my own lab nor this one has been able to identify the organic substance," I explained.

"I don't believe it's the Xathi," Leena continued, "but to be safe, I'm going to run these samples against the data I've collected on those stupid bugs."

"I think that would give everyone some peace of mind," I agreed. She pulled up the chemical analysis of the organic material, as well as the results of several studies I didn't recognize.

"What are those?" I asked, stepping closer to the console.

"My own studies. I have them uploaded to an archive that I can access anywhere," she explained. She pulled up several chemical studies centered around the Xathi. None of them matched the profile of the organic substance found in the craters.

"Well, at least we know what it's not." I ran a hand through my hair.

"I'd almost prefer it if it were the Xathi," Leena sighed. "That's a beast we already know how to fight. There is something interesting, though."

"What's that?" I asked.

"The organic material is not from a Xathi, but it came into contact with a toxic substance recovered from pieces of the Xathi ship," Leena explained. "There are the tiniest traces of it mixed into the soil." She pointed to a group of compounds on the analysis that weren't familiar to me.

"That makes sense. That's the sample that came from out in the desert," I told her. "The planet's crust was thinner in that area. I think the final impact of the pieces of the ship colliding with the planet's surface cracked the crust and fell into that hollow spot. We've no idea how deep it does."

"How has no one noticed a massive hollow spot in the planet?" Leena asked.

"That's exactly what I thought!" I exclaimed. "It's a big area, too. The crater was at least a half mile wide."

"How'd you get these samples?" Leena asked.

"I rappelled into the crater with Karzin and another member of his strike team," I explained. "Karzin thought I was joking at first. He saved my life that day. Something came up from below and attacked us."

"How come none of the other strike teams have heard about it?" Leena asked.

"General Rouhr didn't think it was cause for alarm since it was so far away from civilian populations. I think he would rather our energies be spent closer to home," I explained. "At least that was the plan until the incident in Duvest."

"What happened, exactly?" Leena asked. "Axtin didn't know anything about it."

"It was the strangest thing. There were all these mini-craters, just like the one in the desert. Whatever happened was fast and destructive. People died but the ones who were injured or escaped entirely have no memory of what happened," I explained.

"Bullshit," Leena gasped. I decided that I liked Leena.

"Karzin and I asked everyone we could. No one had any idea what did it. These samples are our only clue," I said.

"We have a proper mystery on our hands then." I didn't miss the gleam of excitement in her eyes.

"There's another mystery I've been trying to work out," I said. Leena gave me a curious look.

"What's that?" she asked.

"I've only known Karzin for a few days, but he seems like a good person," I began. "However, when he interacts with the others, like Axtin and General Rouhr, there's obvious tension. I don't understand it. I feel like I'm missing something."

"That's because Karzin refuses to pull his weight nowadays." I was startled by the bluntness of her speech. "Once the Xathi were defeated, Karzin decided his own agenda was more important than helping to rebuild our planet. He's been unreachable until now. I have no idea how General Rouhr got him down to Nyheim, but good for him for doing so."

"What do you mean by his own agenda?" I asked. I felt guilty for being nosy, but if I was going to keep kissing Karzin – and I planned to keep kissing him - I felt that I should know more about him.

"Months ago, General Rouhr told the entire crew that the *Aurora* was not stable enough to take into deep space and it wouldn't be possible for them to return to their respective homeworlds," she explained.

"That must've been quite a shock," I mumbled.

"It was. Karzin was one of the ones who took it the hardest but, at the time, he got his shit together and did what needed to be done," Leena continued.

"That's good, isn't it?"

"Yes. But as soon as the Xathi were wiped out, he returned here to the *Aurora*. He refused to move into one of the cities. He refused to take assignments. Instead, he wanted to find a way to get off this planet."

"You mean, he wants to go home?" I asked.

Leena nodded.

"The Xathi hit their homeworlds hard. Some of the crew know what happened to their families, they know they have nothing to go back to. Others, like Karzin, never received that kind of closure," Leena sighed. "He's spent the last two months doing who knows what trying to find a way to reach his family. I know he's been tinkering with the satellites."

"Do you think there's a chance he could find a way to reach them?" I thought of my own family. There was a time during the Xathi invasion that we were separated. I couldn't get ahold of them, I didn't know if they were dead or alive.

It was the worst time of my life.

"Honestly?" Leena gave me a blank look that was very telling. "No, I don't. However, I've never been an optimist. Axtin is from the same world as Karzin. Axtin's told me stories about when the Xathi first attacked. The planets were devastated, and as far as anyone knows, the war is still going on out there."

"I'd be miserable if I was stuck here and I knew my family was suffering somewhere I couldn't reach," I said in Karzin's defense.

"I felt for him, too, at first," Leena admitted. "My sister and I didn't speak for years before we reconciled. If I lost her now, I would go mad with grief."

"But?" I prompted.

"But all of us lost something during the Xathi invasion. We all lost friends and family. We lost our homes. We lost our sense of safety. Yet, we all carry on because there's a job to do and we're going to do it, damn it! It's not right that Karzin gets a free pass and leaves the rest of us to pick up his slack."

I understood where Leena was coming from. She experienced the same frustration I sometimes felt with Cassie. But the more I thought about it, the more my heart went out to Karzin.

I wanted to find a way to help him.

I wondered if he'd let me.

KARZIN

My eyes burned and my neck hurt from staring at the computer screens. I forced myself to blink, rubbed my eyes, and tried to stretch my neck. The muscles in my neck were tender, and very sore. The pain meds from the med bay had done nothing for me, so I had tricked Fen into opening a rift for me back to Nyheim, and then again back to the ship.

She hadn't been happy with me when I returned, but I waved her off. She was unhappy that I had used the rift to go buy human alcohol, but I needed it to dull the pain in my neck and head. I emptied a bottle, dropped it next to me, and winced a bit at the loud clatter it made bouncing around. I looked back at the screen and squinted to cut down on the bright light.

There was still nothing. Nothing on any of the

visual scans, nothing on the auditory scans, nothing. Nothing. Nothing anywhere. The only thing I'd found was that small asteroid from the night before. I growled at the lack of information, grabbed another bottle, and switched to satellite four in order to manipulate the frequencies again.

I knew that Dax and Axtin had told me that I needed to find something to take my mind away from this so I didn't hurt myself, but I needed to know. There had to be something out there. I couldn't give up searching for it.

"Karzin?" an almost sheepish voice called to me from behind. I turned in my chair to see a slightly blurred version of Annie at the command center doors. Fen was gliding away behind her.

"What is it, Andromeda?" I asked as I turned back to the computer.

I heard her step into the command center. Her footsteps drew nearer as she answered. "I've been looking for you. I thought you were going to introduce me to Leena."

"I'm sorry. I had forgotten about that." I turned my chair around and looked up at her. "Are you ready to go?"

"I already went to her. She's an amazing woman, did you know that?"

I nodded as I turned back around again. "Yes, Leena

has shown herself to be a very capable and intelligent being."

"That she is. She also kind of told me about what you're doing here."

"Of course she did," I snarled. "That woman might be extremely smart, but she has no idea how to keep her ketonsin mouth shut. So," I said, my voice becoming sarcastic and petulant, "what did she tell you?"

"She said that you're searching for a way home, for your family. That's why you and the rest of the team don't talk much anymore."

I spun my chair around and glared at her. "Really? Is that what she said? What else did she say? That I've become obsessive? That I'm abandoning my team for some fruitless search? That I should give up? Is that what she said?"

Before Annie was able to say anything else, I stood up and stepped towards her. "If they want to give up on our people, then that's their prerogative. I won't, and I shouldn't have to be the target of their comments! It's my right to search for my family and I don't care if they count me as a failure or not, I will not give up looking for a way back to my people."

My breath came hard and heavy as I towered over Annie.

She didn't back down, instead stepping towards me, large eyes bright. "They're all worried about you. From what I've heard, you've spent a lot of time in here and you haven't found anything."

"That," I started, then stopped. I sat back down. "That is true. I have yet to find any signs of my home." I put my head down and closed my eyes. The blood pounded in my head and my neck ached.

Annie came up next to me and put her hands on my shoulders. The light squeeze of her hands felt good.

I rotated my head a bit and she started massaging my shoulders and neck as she spoke. "I know the others might think that what you're doing borders on overly obsessive, but I can understand how you feel."

I looked up at her. "How?"

"When all of you first landed here—or, crashed, actually—I was separated from my family for a while."

A pang ran through me. "How long?"

"A few months." She stopped massaging my shoulders and looked down at me, shadows haunting her eyes. "After the ship crashed down, the Xathi left the ship and began attacking people. I had been at work that day, so I had no idea where anyone was. One day of chaos bled into the next. I spent the next few months in hiding, running when I could to try to get away from the Xathi."

She trembled, lost in the memories.

"I had no idea where they were or if they were okay. It hurt me every day to not know."

I wrapped my hand over hers, wanting only to reassure her, but at her touch a wave of rage ran through me.

Rage for what she had been through. The fear that this beautiful creature had to endure. I couldn't believe that I had not known her and couldn't keep her safe. I had been here, and she had been afraid, and I had done nothing.

She came willingly as I pulled her to me. I sat her on my lap and put my arms around her, as if I could shield her from everything she had gone through.

"I will always protect you, Annie."

She looked into my eyes and smiled. "Everything is fine now, you know," she said softly. "I just wanted you to know that I understand what you're going through. I honestly do."

"Then what should I do?" I asked.

"Keep looking, but don't let it take over your life."

I looked down at her little hands, then up at her. I saw no condescension, no judgment, no pity in her eyes. What I saw was real concern and genuine sympathy.

"You are a strong person, Karzin, and I admire you for how dedicated you are in trying to find your family. I would have done the same if I had all this equipment."

Her eyes were wet, and a small tear began to fall as she spoke. "It was hard to see other families come back together, and to see families receive news that their loved ones were gone, it broke my heart. I started thinking about how I would be if I had ever gotten that news. How would I be able to go on? So I mean it when I say that I admire your dedication in what you're doing."

I reached my hand up and gently wiped the tear away. She grabbed my hand and hugged it while I cupped her face. It was almost absurd how big my hand was compared to her tiny little head. If I had wanted to, I could have crushed her skull with my hand, but all I wanted to do was hold her and comfort her.

Her voice broke just a bit. "Just don't let this become the only thing you do. It'll ruin everything else you have."

She was right. I had let this become an obsession. I had pushed the crew, and especially my team, away from me. Dax and Axtin were right. Living, right here, right now, would keep me sane.

The satellites were still up there, constantly monitoring the space around us. The Urai system kept tabs on every signal used and what was found, so if anything was found, I would be able to go back to see what was found, when it was found, where it was found, and what frequency or wavelength it had been found on.

Still cupping her head, I lifted her face to look at me. "Thank you," I said.

"For what?"

"For helping me remember who I'm supposed to be and what I'm supposed to do. So, thank you for that." I tried to give her my most gentle and sincere smile, but I was worried that it just came across as creepy.

She returned my smile, then hugged me. "You're not such a grumpy jerk after all. I knew there was a good guy inside you."

I gently pushed her away. "You're a funny woman if you think I'm a nice person," I joked.

"Eh. You know you are. The grumpy part is just an act, I can tell."

"Whatever you say, Andromeda." I put a little extra emphasis on her real name in order to get a reaction, and I wasn't disappointed.

She pushed away from me and scoffed. "I told you I don't like my full name," she said, her hands on her hips.

"Too bad, because I really like it," I teased. "It makes you make that cute little pouty lip like the one you have now." I pointed at her mouth, finger dangerously close to running over her lip.

"Ah." She put her hand over her mouth, then glared at me. "You really are a jerk." Her smile lessened the blow of the words.

I shrugged, winked, and motioned her to sit. "So I've been told. Want to see how I've been searching? Maybe you'll have an idea that I haven't had."

She sat down, wheeled the chair over, and I started to show her how to manipulate the controls. We went over all of my previous searches, discussed how I had laid out my search grid, and talked about the different things I was looking for.

We spent the next few hours looking, talking, and just enjoying one another's company. She made me smile and made me want to be the man that I used to be before all of this. I had become so singularly obsessed with finding any sign of my people that I had forsaken the people that I had here.

While my family back on Valorn were hopefully still fighting, I had to realize that my family here, the family of Skotans, K'vers, Urai, and even the humans, were still fighting for survival here. So much had happened here and we were still picking up the pieces.

I needed to help them do that.

I wanted Annie to be proud of me for more than just searching for home, and I wanted my team's respect back.

I wanted to be happy again.

And more and more, I wanted Annie.

ANNIE

Karzin walked me to my room, quiet the entire journey.

Once outside my door, he looked at me. And without a word, he bent lower and brought his mouth to mine.

I surrendered myself willingly. On my tiptoes, I wrapped my arms around him as his hands pulled me to him, strong fingers holding me tight against his body as his tongue darted into my mouth, questing, probing.

As he began to move his arms up and down my back, I moaned loudly. His touch turned my entire body to fire.

His hand kneaded my ass, and I curved in to him, caught against his wide chest. Lower, something hard pressed against my belly.

Hard, and unbelievably large.

I pulled my head back, panting, almost dizzy with need.

"Annie," he growled, then shook himself, darkened eyes softening. With a gentle kiss, he reached to open my door.

And walked away.

I was left breathless.

And very, very horny.

With no time constraint, I look a thirty-minute shower and relished every second of it.

And then went to bed, with nothing but thoughts of Karzin on my mind.

I could remember every sensation as he touched me.

I dreamt of him. Vivid dreams of Karzin danced through my night.

Stripping him naked. Licking my way down his hard body. His strong hands on my heated skin. Watching him enter me. Using my body for his pleasure.

And then…holding me close and snuggling me.

When I woke up, I knew I was his.

At some point during the day before, fresh clothes had been placed in the wall closet in the room. They were simple, a pair of black pants and a navy-blue long-sleeved shirt that hugged every curve of my body as if it were made for me.

At first, I assumed Karzin brought them to my room, but I doubted he'd get the sizing right. The more I thought about it, the more I realized I didn't want to know where the clothing came from. I was simply thankful to have clean clothes.

I left my borrowed room and went to the cafeteria. Karzin was there, sitting alone at a table. When he saw me, his expression brightened. He looked much better this morning. His eyes weren't bloodshot, the circles under his eyes had mostly disappeared, and he looked less haggard.

"Good morning!" I said cheerfully.

Karzin stood up and walked over to me.

"I knew you'd be in sooner or later," he grinned.

"How long have you been waiting?" I asked.

"An hour or so," he shrugged.

"I would've been down sooner if the water pressure in the showers wasn't so divine." We grabbed plates and began filling them with everything laid out before us.

"You should've told me. I would've joined you." Karzin winked and I almost dropped my plate. A blush heated my cheeks. I took a sip of coffee to hide it, which was a terrible idea since it was still scalding hot. I swallowed with difficulty.

"You all right?" Karzin asked with a knowing smile.

"Peachy," I replied. I hurried to a table and set my plate down.

"Did you and Leena have a breakthrough yesterday?" He slid into the seat beside me instead of the one across from me. Our arms brushed together as we ate.

"We've officially ruled out the Xathi. They had nothing to do with our little mishap in the crater. However, a toxic substance from their ship seeped into the soil. There could be something there," I replied.

"That's a relief, I suppose," Karzin nodded. Before he could say anything else, his comm unit starting beeping and buzzing. He pulled it out of his pocket and activated it.

"Yes?" he spoke.

"Karzin, take the geologist and get to Malvor immediately." I recognized General Rouhr's voice.

"She's with me now. What's happened?" Karzin asked.

"There's been another incident. Same as the last time in Duvest. Get down there now!" The comm unit disconnected. Karzin rose from his seat.

"Sorry to cut breakfast short." He gathered up our plates and placed them in a bin filled with dirty dishes.

"Did the general say how bad it is?" I asked.

Karzin shook his head, and I worried.

Malvor was like Somerst, a new settlement propped up by pieces of debris, barely holding itself together. It couldn't handle damage the way Duvest could.

"I know you're not going to like it, but we have to get there now."

"That means traveling by rift, doesn't it?" I winced. Karzin nodded. "Fine. It's an emergency."

We ran from the hall. As we ran, Karzin asked Fen to open a rift for him. I was curious about the device that was able to open and close rifts at will.

It was ready for us, bright and shimmering, when Karzin and I stepped off the *Aurora* and onto the ground. He let me go first. I ducked through as quickly as I could, but that still didn't stop the chill from seeping into my bones. Karzin slipped through after me. Fen closed the rift behind us.

Malvor was in a terrible state. Whole buildings had been toppled and torn apart. People were lying about in various states of injury. There were several dead among them, more than there had been in Duvest. This wasn't going to be easy for Malvor to recover from.

And just as they had in Duvest, craters dotted the ground. Perfectly circular, no cracking in the earth, and no trace of whatever caused them.

"What happened?" Karzin asked the nearest onlooker.

"I don't know," she sniffled. She was coated in a fine layer of dust, but was otherwise uninjured. "Everything was fine. It was a normal day and then suddenly everything was destroyed and people were dead!"

"Just like last time," I whispered. We asked a few more people and received the same response. No one had any idea what had done this.

"How is that possible?" Karzin asked, clearly frustrated.

"I don't know." I placed a hand on his shoulder. "We have to focus on helping people now. We can ponder the mystery of it later." He nodded in agreement.

Malvor didn't have a doctor in town, so Karzin called Dr. Parr on her comm unit. Within minutes, she was standing beside us next to a rift.

"Good to see you again," she nodded to me before rushing to the side of the most severely injured civilian. A building had fallen on top of him, crushing his legs. I had to look away. Noticing my discomfort, Karzin placed a hand on my lower back.

"How about you collect more samples?" he suggested.

I nodded and hurried away from Dr. Parr and the injured man.

While I was in the *Aurora's* lab, I had taken the opportunity to replenish my supplies. This time, I had more vials to collect samples. I could take two for every crater. Hopefully, it would give me a better idea of what had dislodged the soil.

I stepped over to the closest crater and peered down. Like the large one out in the desert, I couldn't see the bottom of these. I started to think that crater wasn't an appropriate term anymore. Tunnel seemed more appropriate.

But a tunnel that came straight up?

"Karzin?" I called.

He came jogging over. "Do you have more of those glow things?"

"You mean the things you called useless?" He folded his arms across his chest.

"Yes, can I borrow a useless glow thing?" I asked again.

"Will I get it back?"

"Probably not," I laughed.

Karzin reached into his pocket and pulled out an already activated glowing rod.

"You had it ready?"

"I guessed that you'd want to toss it into one of the holes," he replied.

I took it from him and did just that. Just like the crater in the desert, the glowing light disappeared into the darkness. If there was a bottom to this crater, it was miles down.

"Now go get it," Karzin nudged me gently.

"Do my eyes deceive me?" A voice caught both our attentions. Walking down the main road of the town was a group of aliens.

As they came closer, I recognized them as the ones

who accompanied me when I first went to investigate the crater. Rouhr must've sent the rest of Strike Team Two as backup.

"Hard to say. You were always a bit blind, Sylor," Karzin joked.

"What the skrell happened here?" a Skotan asked.

"That's what she's trying to figure out," Karzin jerked his head in my direction.

"It's nice to see you all again," I smiled. Each nodded in return.

"Let's focus on getting these people somewhere where the buildings aren't going to come down on their heads," Karzin said decisively. Knowing what I knew now, I expected more push back from his team. However, they seemed happy to oblige. I saw Karzin's features relax noticeably as he fell into rhythm with them.

"Karzin," I called to him. "Hand me your comm unit, please."

"Are you going to throw it into a hole?" he asked.

"No, I'm going to call my father and see if Finola will be willing to take a few people," I explained. He pulled out his comm unit and entered my Dad's contact before tossing it to me.

"Annie, is that you?" my father answered.

"Yes, it's me. I'm working. There's been an accident

and some people need shelter. Can you ask Finola if she'll help?"

"An accident?" I heard my mother squawk in the background. "What kind of accident? Is my baby hurt? What happened?"

"I'm fine, Mom!" I called, though that didn't do much to calm her.

"How many people?" my father asked over my mother.

"As many as Finola can take," I replied.

"Can they pay? You know how Finola is," my father said.

"I'll pay." Karzin appeared at my side. "Tell Finola her green friend has them covered."

"You got it. Send them our way." Feeling satisfied, I clicked off the comm unit and passed it back to Karzin.

"That's so sweet of you to offer to pay for them." I squeezed his arm with appreciation.

"It's the least I can do. Their homes have been destroyed twice now," Karin shrugged.

"Does this mean we have our strike team leader back?" A Skotan approached Karzin with a skeptical look.

"Only if you're ready to help me figure out how to fight an enemy no one sees and no one remembers," Karzin replied.

The Skotan gave him a satisfied smile. “That could be interesting.”

“We could set up cameras,” the K’ver suggested.

“Not bad but they won’t do us much good if they get destroyed in the process,” Karzin replied. “From what I can tell, these attacks happen quickly. Emergency response should be a priority until we get a better idea of what we’re fighting.”

“I think we’ve got to ask the old Skotan for advice,” Sylor said.

Karzin turned to me. “Come with us, Annie. The general will want to hear what you and Leena found yesterday.” I nodded in agreement.

“Do we have to use a rift?” I asked.

“We have transport units,” one of the Skotans said.

“Thank god,” I sighed.

Once the injured civilians were on their way to Finola, Karzin and his team were ready to go. Karzin offered his hand to me as we walked. I took it and held tight. The other members of the strike team noticed and shared curious looks.

Karzin squeezed my hand.

The warmth made me smile, distracted me from my circling thoughts.

What could be doing this? And how could we stop it?

KARZIN

It was like the darkest days of the war against the Xathi for Ankou. Strike Teams One, Two, and Three all crowded into Rouhr's office, trying to come up with a plan.

But this time the enemy was an enigma.

We knew nothing. Not what it was, how it traveled, what it wanted.

Nothing.

I still received some dirty looks from the other teams, but my team supported me. They knew I was back, and that I had found a way to conquer my addictive obsession with the satellites.

Vrehx still looked like Vrehx, his deep red skin with a few new scars and his military-issued haircut still in place. The difference in him was the look in his eyes.

While still serious, they were now filled with joy and a sense of belonging that I hadn't seen in him before.

Tu'ver sat next to Vrehx, his black skin and green circuitry shining under his white shirt. He had taken to a more informal style of dress since the end of the Xathi, wanting to show himself as less hostile. He, as well, looked less stressed than before, he was smiling and sharing a quiet joke with Vrehx. The smile looked good on him.

Dax and Axtin were polite to me and gave me a good-natured nod when they saw that I was behaving like the old me. Sakev had never been bothered by my actions, so he still treated me as he always had.

It was Team Three that still distrusted me, and I couldn't blame them. Sk'lar, the black-skinned and blue-circuited K'ver, as leader of Team Three, had the biggest reason to distrust me. When I shirked my responsibilities, as the leader of Team Three, it fell to him to take over with Vrehx on leave.

He was professional, but I could feel the icy stares coming from his direction. The rest of his team, Jalok and Cazak—the Skotans, and Tyehn and Navat—my Valorni cousins, followed his lead. They were angry, and while they weren't as angry as Sk'lar, they also didn't show me any sympathy, either.

That was fine. I had earned their scorn and I knew it would take work to get their respect back.

I fully planned on doing just that.

"We need to enlist what's left of the human soldiers to keep an eye on each city, new and old. We need a more reliable word on what is attacking the cities, and I don't think civilians are going to cut it," Rouhr said. He sat at the head of the conference table, while the rest of us filled the chairs down each side.

"I agree, General Rouhr," Sk'lar said. "I would also like to begin a recruiting drive and train more men and women to be able to defend themselves. The better we are able to prepare these humans, the better they will be able to care for themselves when and if we find a way back to our real home."

"This time, Sk'lar, I agree with you. Not for the same reasons, but I agree," Rouhr amended. "The better trained and prepared we can get everyone, the better for all of us." He turned to Vrehx, who was the direct liaison between our people and the human military forces. "Do you think you would be able to speak to them and coordinate things?"

Vrehx nodded. "Yes, sir, I don't believe it will be an issue. And as for Sk'lar's idea, I think this new threat validates his plans. I'll run the ideas past Tona and Skit. They'll know if there are people interested in the military route or not."

Rouhr gave a nod of his own. "Good. If we can get members of our own crew, as well as human soldiers in each settlement, we may be able to not only get information on whatever this is but might be able to have people already on hand to fight it."

He looked around the room. "I hate to do this to everyone, because I know that we all have responsibilities, but I want each team on stand-by until this is taken care of."

No one argued the logic. We needed everyone ready to go at a moment's notice, and that wouldn't work if we were off doing other things. However, it did mean that some of our repair and construction efforts would suffer a bit.

It couldn't be helped, though.

"Here's a question," Sakev cut in. "How do you fight something you can't see, or, apparently, remember? I mean," he looked around the room at everyone, and it seemed as though his gaze settled on me a moment longer than anyone else. "How do you fight something you know absolutely nothing about?"

It was a good question. None of us had seen it. Rokul and I were the only ones that had encountered whatever it was, and neither of us had any information other than it was solid, and potentially slimy.

"Well, we know that whatever is doing this doesn't like light," Sylor said. "According to what Rokul and Karzin told us about their excursion into the big pit, nothing happened until they used the light sticks. To me, that sounds like they have a problem with light."

"Okay, how do we use that?" Rouhr asked. "We can't exactly light up the entire inside of a planet."

"We could send a team underground, have lights attached to battle-suits in order to prevent an attack. Maybe see where they're coming from?" Sylor suggested.

"That's actually not a bad suggestion. Do we have any suits left, though?" Vrehx asked.

"Only my team does," Sk'lar answered. "We had never gotten them off the shuttle before we abandoned the *Vengeance*."

"Does your team volunteer to go down into the crater?" Rouhr asked.

"If necessary, then yes, we do," Sk'lar answered. "What are our contingency plans if we find nothing?" We spent the next few hours coming up with several plans of action, each one based on a different hypothesis of what could be causing all of this. Tobias had brought in water and food for us as we debated.

"So, since we know that these things are organic, do we kill it?" Tu'ver asked.

"Of course, we kill it," Axtin answered. "It's dangerous and it's killing people."

"What if it's not meaning to kill people?" Iq'her mused. "For the amount of damage, the casualty rate is remarkably low. If these were active attacks, I'd expect a higher body count."

General Rouhr coughed.

"Not that I'm complaining," Iq'her hastily added. "Just another mystery." He looked around the table. "What if it's sentient, and not actually attacking with intent to kill?"

That raised an entirely new debate, but before things got heated, the emergency signal rang out.

Rouhr quickly turned on the wall screen. On the screen was Tona, covered in dust and looking a bit battered.

"What's going on, Captain Tona?" Rouhr asked.

The picture shook a bit and Tona looked behind him. He yelled out orders to his people, then turned back to us.

"We've just been attacked in Einhiv, General. We're not sure what the hell happened, but we've got holes popping up in our business district, sir. I've already accounted for four toppled buildings, sir. Each one was occupied. We're already working on search and rescue, but we need help."

"Understood, Captain. We'll send help there immediately. Is there anything you can tell us about what attacked you?"

Tona shook his head and coughed. "No, sir. All anyone remembers is the ground started to shake, then there were holes in the ground. A few people look beat up, but no one remembers getting into a fight with anything. Sir, I need to get back to my people. When can we expect you?"

"As soon as possible, Captain. Rouhr out." The screen clicked off and Rouhr looked at me. "I want you and your team to head over immediately. Grab whatever gear you think you need and have Fen rift you there."

"Sir," I said with a nod. As I stood, Rouhr got onto his comm. "Tobias? Get Doctor Parker on the line, now."

"Sir? What about us?" Vrehx asked.

"As much as I want to send all of you, I need Teams One and Three to remain here in case there's another attack," Rouhr answered. He turned back to me. "I'll send more help as quickly as I can get it coordinated."

"Yes, sir. Gear still in the basement?"

"Affirmative."

I looked at my team. "Let's go." We rushed down to the basement, geared up, and I put in the call to Fen.

"This will be good timing."

"What?" Speech pad malfunction. Had to be. The Urai weren't exactly expressive, but they'd never been hard-hearted.

"I have been integrating the Gateway with the

Aurora's A.I. As I mentioned, I do have other responsibilities."

Oh. She had, hadn't she. And we'd all been treating her like nothing but a glorified shuttle driver.

"That's brilliant, you know."

"Yes, I do. Your rift will be ready momentarily. The A.I. will open it, while I observe."

As we made our way out of the building, I saw Annie running towards us.

"You okay?" I asked as she came up to us.

She spent a second catching her breath, then looked up at me. "Rouhr told me what happened. He wants me to stay in the lab."

"Good. We need all the information we can get. I'll try to get you more samples to test while I'm there," I said.

"Okay. Be careful, please," she said. "I'm worried about you."

I reached down and pulled her close to me. I brought my mouth to hers and gave her a deep kiss. She tasted of heat and desire. It took all my effort to pull away.

"I will keep your taste to remind me of you. And I will be careful, promise. Now, go. Rouhr is going to want all the information you can find, even if you've already gone over it a dozen times already."

I let her go and joined my team as the rift opened.

"At least you're smiling," Sylor smirked. His eyes showed mirth, so I didn't punch him.

"Shut up and move," I ordered. We went through the rift and exited outside the west gates of Einhiv. Looked like the AI would be just fine at the job.

We were ushered in and rushed to where the destruction was. It looked bad, and terribly familiar.

"Hey!" Tona called out to us from a pile of rubble close to a nine-foot-wide crater. We rushed over and got to work.

ANNIE

I didn't like the idea of Karzin and his team going without me. I knew there wasn't anything I could do to help the people of Einhiv. In fact, I'd probably slow Karzin and his team down if I tagged along. Not knowing what was happening made me uneasy.

What if Karzin arrived and the attack was still going on? Would he remember? Would he be injured?

I dragged myself out of General Rouhr's base of operations to walk to my own lab. Leena had saved all of my data in her personal archive and gave me an access code so I could pull it up in my lab.

Still, I didn't know how I'd be able to concentrate knowing Karzin was somewhere else, possibly putting himself in danger.

"You all right, Annie?" Orlin called from his shack. He had a line of people waiting to order.

"It's been a hell of a week, Orlin," I called back.

"Your sister came to see me," Orlin said. I stopped dead in my tracks.

"What?" I turned and walked back to the shack, stepping in front of other patrons.

"Yeah, she wanted a job."

"Did you give her one?" I asked.

"I agreed to a trial period. It's obvious the girl hasn't worked a day in her life," Orlin explained.

"I'll say," I mumbled. "I appreciate it, Orlin. If she works out, it'll be a huge help for the family."

"That's why I did it," Orlin grinned. "You're like family. You remind me so much of my daughter."

I felt a lump grow in my throat. Orlin's daughter died here in Nyheim when the Xathi first attacked.

"Thanks so much, Orlin. I'll be by soon for breakfast." I waved to him as I continued on in the direction of my building.

I tried to imagine Cassie working at Orlin's place. I couldn't picture it, even though it was what I'd wanted all along. If I made it home tonight, I wouldn't say anything about it. Cassie didn't like it when people made a big fuss over her, contrary to what her personality would have someone believe. She was a bit of an enigma, but I loved her all the same.

When I entered the building, Bea was upon me in an instant.

"Where have you been?" she demanded. "It's not like you to miss more than a day. Is someone sick? Are you sick? Don't get me sick! I still have so much to do before I leave."

"Back on the caffeine pills are you, Bea?" I asked, not breaking stride. I entered the elevator. Bea followed.

"I was never off them," she replied. "Your equipment has gone silent again. Shame. For a moment there, I thought you were on to something."

"I am, actually." I kept my gaze straight ahead. "I can't say much about it without General Rouhr's permission." I didn't know if that was true or not, but if it got Bea off my back, I'd roll with it.

"Is that so?" she gasped. "I've heard so much about the general. Is he really as frightening as the stories make him out to be?"

"He has a strong presence," I said, which wasn't a lie. He did.

"Have you been working with the aliens all this time?" Bea asked. The elevator dinged and the doors opened.

"I'm sorry, Bea. I can't say anything more about it," I breezed off the elevator, hoping she wouldn't follow me. Thankfully, she didn't. She didn't even step off the elevator. I think she only hopped on just to continue pestering me.

I unpacked the samples from Malvor and ran them through my equipment. My computer still couldn't identify anything, but it could give me a rough analysis. When compared to the ones saved in Leena's archive, I could see the Malvor samples were nearly identical to the other samples I'd already taken.

Obviously, whatever came out of the craters in Duvest was the same as whatever came out of the craters in Malvor. I didn't need my lab to tell me that. What I needed to know was what was coming out of those craters. I wouldn't figure that out by staring at little piles of dirt. I needed more.

I needed to go back to the large crater.

Karzin would never agree to it after what happened last time. Or worse, he'd agree to go but refuse to take me along. I didn't want him to go into the desert again. If anything happened to him, I didn't know how I would handle it.

I'd go alone.

I'd go quickly and quietly, and be back before anyone knew I was gone. Besides, I'd have a better chance of rappelling into the crater unnoticed if I went alone and didn't use any lights.

I drummed my fingers on the lab bench. I'd still

need someone to watch my ropes from the surface and pull me up in case of an emergency.

I looked around the lab at the other scientists working at their stations. I didn't know any of them very well. I'd only been working here a little over a month. To them, I was the bottom-rung new girl. I wasn't in a position to ask favors yet, especially dangerous ones.

Then, out of the corner of my eye, I spied him. An intern.

I smothered a manic smile as I approached him. He was tall, at least six feet, but as skinny as a bean pole. His dark hair was in need of a trim. He smiled eagerly.

"Lennox, right?" I asked him. He nodded vigorously. "What are you working on currently?"

"I was just going to prepare samples for Dr. Wilks to test." Lennox looked over at the portly old scientist, who was half asleep at his station.

"He's got you doing all of his work while he naps? Despicable," I laughed. Lennox gave me a nervous smile. "I'm working on something important for General Rouhr, and I could really use an assistant."

"You're the geologist, right?" he asked. "I don't think I'd be much help. I specialized in neurology."

"That's okay!" I said brightly. "You don't need to know anything to help me with this."

"I really should get those samples taken care of." He started to walk away, but I grabbed his arm.

"Did I tell you I'm going out in the field? Where the pieces of the Xathi ship fell?"

His eyes brightened with interest.

"I've always wanted to see that ship up close," he said.

"Now's your chance. Plus, General Rouhr has a special interest in this project. I'll give you credit for everything you do." I had him on the hook. He glanced nervously at Dr. Wilks. "I doubt Dr. Wilks will mention you in his final report."

That did the trick.

"What do you need from me?" Lennox asked.

"First, we're going to check out some climbing equipment." His expression was overcome with worry. "Don't worry, you won't be doing any of the climbing," I assured him.

No one paid us any mind as we left the lab. One floor below us was a room stocked with equipment for fieldwork. I signed out climbing boots with spikes, plenty of rope, a harness with extra reinforcement, and anything else I thought I might need.

"I've never done any field work before," Lennox said excitedly as I passed him two duffel bags full to bursting.

"How exciting for you!" I said. "It's really important work, too. You'll be glad to have helped."

"What are we doing, exactly?" he asked. I considered him a moment before deciding there was no harm in telling the kid the truth.

Part of the truth, at least.

"I went out to the desert a few days ago to check on some unusual readings," I explained. "When I got there, I found this huge crater. Now I'm thinking it might be a tunnel. It's incredibly deep. Miles deep. I didn't get a chance to collect enough samples last time I was out there. Today, I'll rappel down deeper and get better samples." I decided to leave out the part where Karzin and I nearly died.

I didn't want to frighten the poor kid.

"What are you hoping to learn?" he asked.

"The planet's crust in that specific area is thin. That's why the debris from the Xathi ship was able to cause a collapse. I want to figure out why the crust is so thin," I explained.

"Why?" he asked.

"What if the crust is thin in other places?" I asked. "What if Nyheim is one crack away from falling into the center of the planet?"

"Then why aren't you testing here?" Lennox asked. I sucked in a deep breath. I really didn't want to tell him about the attacks, but if he kept this up, I wouldn't have a choice.

"Because there isn't a crater here," I replied. "Come on, we're wasting time! I want to get back long before nightfall."

"How are we getting there?"

Crap.

That was a valid question. The office had a single land-based transport unit available to scientists to use for field work, but the project had to be preapproved in advanced. I wasn't officially working on a project. I'd been thrown into this and never drew up a project report. I'd been too busy leaping through rifts and kissing a green alien.

"We're going to ask nicely," I said with a decisive nod.

The lab director was in her office, looking over papers no doubt filled with properly submitted project outlines.

"Doctor Parker," she said without looking up. "General Rouhr sent me a message about you, commending you for all of your help. I'm glad I sent you to him."

"So am I, Dr. Hines," I smiled. "I actually came here to ask you about that."

"Oh?"

"General Rouhr and I are still working together.

He's asked me to collect more samples. Naturally, he didn't realize I needed to submit a project outline to get approval to use the transport unit. If no one's using it, can I borrow it for a few hours?"

I held my breath as she pondered.

"If it's for the general's work, all right," she nodded. I let out a sigh of relief.

"Thank you. I'll be sure to tell the general how helpful you were."

Before Dr. Hines could say another word, I pushed Lennox out of the office and made a break for the garage.

KARZIN

The scene at Einhiv was terrible. We had spent hours fishing survivors, and non-survivors, out of the rubble of two buildings while people worked in the other two buildings that had fallen.

Of the four buildings that had fallen, two of them were still mostly intact, they had fallen because their foundations had been compromised. For the third building, the top half of it broke off and crumbled into the street, killing one pedestrian.

The fourth building, the building Tona had directed us to, was the worst. Not only had it fallen over, but part of it had fallen into a nearby crater. Our only saving grace was that the crater wasn't very wide, or very deep.

We had noticed that there were two types of craters.

There were the ones with bottoms that we could see. And ones that went on forever.

We were on a break, trying to get as much rest as we could so we wouldn't make a mistake. Someone had brought us some water, and I sat on a set of stairs, watching the rescue efforts commence as the sun came back up over the horizon. I was sore, and I think I had lost skin from one of my shins, but I was encouraged by what I was seeing. The people of Einhiv had come together and were working nonstop to get as many people out as they could, while cleaning up as much rubble as possible to help make room for the rescue.

Tona came to sit next to me. "Thank you for coming. I was kind of expecting the other teams as well, though."

I took a drink of water and nodded. "The general wanted to keep the other teams on standby just in case another attack happened somewhere. He did, however, send the two shuttles with supplies and extra help."

"Yeah, I sincerely appreciate that. Sorry, just tired."

"It's okay. How are you?" I asked. I liked Tona. He was a good man. I would not worry about going into combat with him by my side.

He let out a sigh that seemed to come from his ancestors. "Exhausted, in pain, and my lungs are probably filled with dust, but I'm here."

"Has anyone said anything about whether or not

they saw anything?"

He shook his head. "No. Most of the people coming out are asking us what happened. No one knows anything, and that bothers me."

"You and me both."

"Were you wanting to look at the craters? I know you need to get as much info as you can."

I nodded. "If you can spare us, but we're more than willing to jump back in and help."

"Honestly?"

"Please."

"This crew is about dead on their feet. You think you can help me finish up?" he asked as he stood and extended his hand to me.

"Let's get to work." I accepted his hand and let him pull me up. "Let's get back to it, boys."

The team got to their feet without complaint and we went back to work. The few hours turned into half the day before we found everyone.

Although there were only six dead, that was six too many. I ordered everyone to get some sleep. We needed the rest before we looked into the craters. While the team went to find a place to rest, I went to one of the craters to have a look.

This one wasn't big, maybe ten feet deep and six feet across. I called over one of the rescue workers and asked him to get my rappelling gear. When he returned with my gear, I had already gotten a ladder and put it down into the pit. I put on my gear, attached myself to a street post, and headed for the ladder.

"Why did you need your gear if you have the ladder?" he asked me.

"Simple. If the floor of the crater isn't strong enough to hold my weight, I'll fall through, and I don't know how far I'll fall. If it does break underneath me, the rope will catch me as long as the street post is solid."

"Ah. Makes sense. I'm here if you need me, sir."

"Appreciate that," I said as I stepped onto the ladder. I gingerly made my way down, taking soil samples for Annie along the way. When I got to the bottom of the crater, I slowly stepped off the ladder, testing the ground with my foot. It held.

The crater was a tight fit, but I managed. I took a sample of the soil I was standing on, then twisted around the bottom of the crater, trying to see if I could find anything useful. I searched the whole of the crater, finding nothing, at first.

"Ho, Karzin!" a voice called to me from above. I glanced up to see a short, well-built man looking down. It took a moment for me to remember who it was.

"Ho, Skit," I called back.

"Find anything?"

"Not yet," I answered as I looked down again. I noticed something that time. Some of the dirt seemed to be falling in on itself. I knelt down to get a closer look.

"There's something you need to look at over here," Skit said.

"Okay. Just a minute." I dug a bit into the spot and the dirt came away quickly and easily. Then I noticed a small hole in the crater wall. The dirt began falling through faster and faster. I got to my feet and ran for the ladder, but the ground gave way beneath me. I slammed into the wall of the crater as the ladder fell another twenty feet in a rain of dirt and debris.

"Oh, shit!" I heard Skit yell. My rope tautened and then I was being pulled upwards. "Are you alright?" he asked me as I was pulled back to the surface.

I took a few moments to catch my breath before I nodded. I rolled over to the edge of the crater and looked down. I could see the ladder at the bottom, and what looked to be small tunnels. "Well, whatever it is that's doing this, now we know how they're moving around."

"Yeah." Skit looked at me and I looked at him, then both of us put stupid grins on our faces at the thought that I had nearly died because of dirt.

"You said you had something to show me?" I asked.

He nodded. "Yeah, it's actually at the bigger crater, but you've already seen it. I was going to show you that we had found tunnels."

"Oh, well, then I'm glad I could save you the trouble," I quipped.

"Huh. I thought Sakev was the only one that had that stupid sense of humor."

"Ouch. Okay, I'll just get to my investigation now," I said as I rolled to my feet.

Skit helped me up, then looked up at me. "I didn't say it was a bad thing." With that, he turned and left to go back to whatever it was that Tona needed him to do. I moved about the area, looking at each of the craters and trying to see where they had materialized.

"I can't tell if it's on purpose or just random." I turned to see Sylor standing close by.

"I thought I ordered you to get some rest," I said.

He shrugged. "You never said how much," he returned. "So, do you think it's deliberate?"

"I don't know." I answered. "It seems as if the dead here, Malvor, and Duvest were all the result of either falling into the crater or having something fall on them. Even though it looked like someone was beaten to death in Malvor, I'm not sure it was entirely malicious."

"Really?"

"Think about it. All of this damage looks almost incidental, even accidental in nature. I'm wondering how we can be sure if whatever this is is doing it on purpose," I said. "We still need samples from each hole. If you're up for it, grab your gear and get some."

"Aye, aye, sir." He snapped me a salute, his way of being sarcastic, and jogged away to where our gear had been stored.

I wondered if I was right.

Was this all accidental or was it on purpose? Was this a sentient being, or beings, trying to scare us away, or trying to hurt us?

I needed to talk to Annie, see what she thought. I called her building and I was transferred to her lab.

No answer.

A feeling gnawed at me. Almost as if it was a warrior's instinct.

There was something wrong with Annie.

I tried again to call her. No answer again.

I could feel an instinct telling me there was something wrong with my mate.

I couldn't explain it.

I just knew.

I called the building and this time asked if she was there. The person that answered didn't know, so they transferred me to another line in Annie's lab. A woman answered.

"Yes?"

"Hello. Is Annie Parker currently available?" I asked.

"She's not here," was the reply.

"Can you tell me where she might be? If you know, of course."

The woman on the line blew air into the receiver. "I have no idea where she is," she said. The tone of her voice told me that she didn't want to be bothered. "All I know is that she grabbed some intern, some equipment, and left. Damn woman, shirking her duties around here," she finished as if she were talking to herself and forgot she was on the line with me.

"Uh, thank you, ma'am. I appreciate it." I hung up. What could she possibly be working on? Why would she need…

Oh, skrell.

There was only one reason why she needed to leave the lab and take equipment with her.

She was going to ground zero. She was heading back to the original crater, and she had gotten someone to go with her.

Of all the asinine, impulsive…she was going to get hurt. Something terrible popped into my head as I thought of her actions.

What if the small craters were created by small creatures? That would mean the big one, the one that went down nearly half a mile or more…what made that one?

I had to get to her, and fast. "Sylor!" I yelled. Time for him to step up.

Annie needed me.

ANNIE

Lennox hadn't stopped gawking at the pieces of the Xathi ship, which was fine with me. It gave me the chance to do my work in peace. I took samples of the earth from around the ship fragments where I'd found the liquid residue. It was likely that it was the same toxic substance Leena detected when she'd looked at the samples.

She didn't have very much information on it, so at least these samples could help further her research if they didn't prove useful to mine.

I recalled something Dr. Parr said when I was in her practice. She told me to contact a woman called Jeneva if I wanted to find out more about strange things happening on the planet. I'd been in such a rush since then that I'd completely forgotten. Perhaps I should've talked to her before charging out here, but so much was happening, and so quickly, I'd forgotten.

Oh, well. I was already here. Not much I could do about that now.

"It's time to set up the climbing equipment," I called to Lennox. He popped out from behind a piece of the Xathi ship that was almost the size of my house.

Lennox didn't do very much to help me set up. I tied all the knots and secured the anchor. I clipped myself into the harness and showed Lennox what to look for if something were to go wrong.

"Are you sure you understand everything?" I asked him for the third time.

"Yes," Lennox insisted. "It's not that complicated. You're acting like you're expecting something to go wrong."

"I just like to know that the stranger I've entrusted with my life is up to the job," I replied.

"I'm a Ph.D. candidate, I can handle a few ropes," Lennox insisted. "If you're so worried about working with a stranger, why *are* you working with me?"

"Less cheek, please," I scolded. "Dr. Hines knows you're with me. If anything happens to me, she'll know you had something to do with it. So, if saving my life isn't enough of a motivator, think about saving your internship."

Lennox actually paled at the prospect.

"Yes, ma'am," he murmured.

"That's much better." I never thought I'd be the one to bully an intern. I'd feel guiltier if my life wasn't on the line.

"Are those night vision goggles?" Lennox asked, nodding to my bag.

"Yes." I grabbed them and put them in place on my forehead.

"Can't you just use a flashlight?" he asked.

"If I could use a flashlight, don't you think I'd be using a flashlight?" I retorted.

"Right. But why can't you?" he asked.

"I need you to stop with the questions," I sighed as I clipped the rope to my harness.

"I'm an intern. I'm supposed to ask questions," Lennox replied.

"Not when I'm lowering myself backward into a bottomless abyss." I leaned back, doing everything in my power not to look over my shoulder. Before I started lowering myself, I looked at Lennox.

"This is going to sound weird, but please don't question it. Once I start going down, do not talk to me. No questions, no wonderings. Don't even talk to yourself. If you have an urge to shine a light down into the hole, resist the urge. If you're worried about me, do not call for me. If something is wrong, you will know.

Most importantly, I don't know how long I'll be down there. So, if you get bored and decide to walk away, you better hope I don't find out about it. I won't throw you into the abyss, but I know someone who will. Got it?"

Lennox opened his mouth to speak but then quickly snapped it closed. He nodded vigorously. He'd already been pale, now he looked positively translucent.

"Good lad," I nodded. I took a deep, shuddering breath before taking my first steps down into the crater. I took one or two more samples from the areas Karzin and I'd already covered, but I soon moved farther down.

The light disappeared quickly. I switched on the night vision goggles. I'd never used the gear before and could've been using them incorrectly, but I could see well enough, so it would have to do. Now that I was suspended in total darkness and perfect silence, I felt safer.

Last time, nothing happened to us until Karzin turned on the light. That might've simply been a coincidence, but I wasn't prepared to take that chance. Whatever was down here didn't seem to care when Karzin dropped his glowstick.

Or maybe it was just earth. There was so much I didn't know stacked before me like a mountain. But not a mountain of solid earth, it was a mountain of sand.

Every time I tried to get a foothold, I slipped farther down.

My head felt clumsy and heavy as I looked around with the night vision goggles. My neck began to ache. If Dr. Parr knew I was down here before my back was healed, she'd kill me. No, Dr. Parr was too kind for that. She'd probably tell me she was very disappointed in me, which would be worse.

Hell, if Karzin knew I was down here, he'd be furious. He'd probably shoot something.

My mind began to wander, thinking of the various ways I could distract him from being angry. Maybe I'd run my hands down his sides, explore the broad planes of his chest. Maybe I'd be brave, kiss my way down his belly.

Even go further.

And he'd forget all about being mad at me for being down here.

With a shake of my head, I tried to clear my thoughts and focus. My thoughts were racing out of control. I couldn't put a stop to them. My heart rate was picking up as I sunk lower and lower. I needed to get ahold of myself. I couldn't work properly if I let thoughts of Karzin distract me.

I reached out and touched the side of the crater. To my surprise, the earth felt damp and cool to the touch. I paused to fill a few vials with samples. When my tiny scooper broke the earth, the air around me filled with a familiar, almost comforting, smell. It smelled just like soil after a week of rain.

As lush as this planet's natural forests were, we didn't get much rain. Like desert plants, our jungle plants had evolved to retain water. Their roots ran deep to siphon water from the streams that flowed through the forest. Those streams were the result of natural wells deep below the surface of the earth. Perhaps I was near one of them now. Hopefully not very close, I wouldn't want a well to burst on top of me while I was down here, unable to escape anything.

I clamped my lips together as I tried not to laugh at the image that suddenly popped into my head. I thought of poor Lennox, returning to the office to tell Dr. Hines that I died in the field while rappelling down into a crater. Then I imagined her asking how it happened only to hear that, of all things, I'd drowned.

Something must've been seriously wrong with me if I found that funny. It had to be nerves.

Get yourself together, I scolded myself. I lowered myself down another twenty feet. Above me, the light of the sky looked so far away. I decided I didn't want to know the exact distance I'd traveled.

I fought the urge to hum to myself like I often did when I worked alone. Instead, I focused on my breathing to keep my heart rate slow and steady. I took a deep inhale through my nose. The cloying, damp smell grew more intense.

If I closed my eyes and relied only on my sense of smell, I would think I was standing in the middle of the jungle. The smell was so earthy, but it was more than that. I could smell greenery and moss. Perhaps, I actually had found one of the wells. I didn't know why there would be one in a barren desert.

I took more samples, hoping that I would get even a tiny bit of whatever was causing that mossy, green smell. As I collected my samples, I thought about Karzin. I wondered if he was back from Einhiv yet. I hoped the damage wasn't too bad.

As I hung suspended above endless black, I realized that I missed him. I wanted him here with me and not just because I was starting to feel nervous about being down here alone. Even if he couldn't joke and laugh with me, I wanted him here.

I'd kiss him when I saw him next. He'd surprised me with that kiss in the mess hall. I wanted to repay him in kind.

I felt something vibrate through my rope. Dragging my thoughts away from Karzin, I looked up. The night vision goggles made it impossible to get a good look at what was happening above me. I took a deep breath and told myself Lennox accidentally bumped the anchor or twanged the rope. I was fine.

Everything was fine.

It was time for me to head back up. I had plenty of samples to examine when I returned to my lab. If I asked Karzin, I bet he would take me back to the *Aurora* so I could use the lab there.

If I was being honest with myself, I was starting to feel afraid. I didn't want to be down in this dark pit anymore. I wanted to be wherever Karzin was. When I thought of safety, I thought of him. I'd ask him to dinner when I got back to General Rouhr's main office.

I began the slow process of working my way up the rope. Suddenly, I felt a stinging pain in my ankle. I barely had time to process it when I felt a slash on the back of my leg. It felt like I was being beaten with a whip of stinging nettles.

"Lennox!" I screamed. "Pull me up!"

I was so far down I wasn't sure if he could hear me.

I kicked my leg, trying to free myself. I came into contact with something solid and moving. I pulled up with all my might, trying to get back to daylight, as if the rays of the sun would save me.

For a moment, I felt nothing. I let myself believe that I'd fought off whatever it was that had whipped me.

Then I felt it again. It came up from below.

Something ropey and slightly damp wrapped around my ankle.

I kicked and kicked but couldn't shake it a second time.

I looked up with horror as I realized I was being pulled down, away from the light.

KARZIN

I had to get to Annie.

That was the only thought in my head.

Rokul knew how to take and bag samples, Sylor knew what to look for, and Iq'her and Takar would follow orders. They were going to be fine.

Even with the help of the A.I. Fen was unable to open a rift for me. They were slammed moving refugees. I raced to find Tona.

"I need a shuttle, a fast one," I said when I found him. When he looked at me questioningly, I lied and told him that Annie had called for help at the original crater.

He took me to a small garage two blocks away and opened it. Inside were two small shuttles, each of them painted to represent the Einhiv security force. He quickly powered one up for me.

"Thank you," I said as I jumped in.

"Just make sure I get it back," he said, then quickly added, "in one piece!" I gave him a quick salute and took off. The controls were simple, and I had the shuttle racing across the countryside towards the *Aurora* and the original crater as fast as it would go.

All I could think of, because of the small tunnels we had found, was that Annie was in more trouble than she could possibly handle and that I would be too late.

I pushed the little shuttle to its limits. Everything flew by me in a blur of greens and browns, then just brown as I flew over the desert. I was nearly in a full panic by the time I flew over the *Aurora*.

All I could imagine was Annie, dying or dead, and I hadn't been there to protect her.

There it was. The crater that had started it all, and a shuttle parked a few yards away from it. I didn't see Annie, but I saw someone else standing there, struggling with her guide line. The intern. I set the shuttle down in a hurry and rushed out.

"Help us," the thin young man yelled as I ran over. I was about to ask what was wrong, when I heard Annie scream and saw her line move erratically.

Instinct took over where thought would have

slowed me down. I attached my own rappel line to the anchor they used, tied my rope off, and dove.

As I fell, I saw Annie kicking at something as she was being swung and bounced around against the crater walls.

I utilized my brake, stopped falling, and ran on the wall of the crater over to her. Something tripped me and I sort of 'fell' and stumbled my way to her. I was able to regain my awkward balance just before I crashed into her.

"Karzin! Something has my leg." She was terrified and nearly hysterical.

I looked down, but it was too dark here, her head was the only thing in the light, and the shadows were growing.

I nodded to her and pulled out my knife as I dropped another couple of feet into the darkness. I felt around, found her leg, and dragged my hand down her leg.

Nothing. I had grabbed the wrong leg. I reached for the other one and found something was wrapped around her calf and ankle. I couldn't cut there or else I would cut her, so I dropped down another foot and started cutting whatever it was that was holding her.

Whatever it was, it was hard, almost scaly. Not scaly like a Skotan, or what the humans called snakes, but it felt as if there were pieces of the thing on top of itself. It was almost like a tentacle, or a root, or maybe even a vine, but thick and very tough to cut through.

"HURRY!" I heard her yell from above me. Something slapped me in the back, but I wouldn't stop. I continued to cut and saw at the thing. The more I sawed through whatever this tentacle was, the more I was being battered by another one or two on my back and legs.

I finally cut through it, felt something on my hands as I did, and climbed up a bit. Another, smaller tentacle had wrapped itself into Annie's gear and was shaking her. I grabbed her in order to stabilize her and something hit me hard in the back of the head. All I could see for a few precious seconds were stars and tiny explosions of light. I blinked them away as I struggled to steady Annie enough for me to cut the tentacle from her gear.

I grabbed it, found a part of it that wasn't in her gear or on her, and cut, stabbed, and sawed through that one, as well. It didn't take as long this time, it didn't feel as thick. As I finished cutting it off, all of the tentacles fell away from us. We were in total darkness and silence, the only sounds were our own labored breathing, then suddenly it wasn't.

Rocks were falling and tumbling down below us as something was smacking into the crater walls, and it was getting closer. “It’s climbing towards us,” I whispered in wonder.

I grabbed Annie and pulled her up behind me. She had gotten her wits together enough to climb and we did, as fast as we could, as the sounds below us got louder, closer, and more menacing. We made it to the part of the crater that still had light, which gave us hope and energy, helping us to climb even faster.

Something hit my leg, tried to wrap around me, but I kicked at it and propelled myself to the side, away from it. I climbed further, then swung myself back over towards Annie as I saw something coming out of the darkness to grab her. As I swung by, I cut at it with my knife and it pulled away, no sound other than our own desperate scrambling and the boy above us screaming for us to hurry.

Annie reached the top and he helped pull her over the edge and away. He was half dragging, half helping her away from the edge when I got there and rolled over myself. I scrambled from the edge of the crater and looked back, but saw nothing.

I heard the sounds of it retreating back into the hole, strange, terrifying. The massive size of whatever that was, at least in my imagination, was daunting.

I looked back at Annie to see her struggling to catch her breath, the intern stretched on his back next to her.

“We’re okay,” I said. “We’re okay. It’s gone.” I tried to

catch my own breath, using the technique that Vrehx had taught us.

I cleared my mind, focused on Annie, and forced myself to take deep breaths. She had been watching me and must have decided to mimic me, for her own breathing slowed down, as well.

And as the panic, fear, and utter terror began to fade away, it was replaced with worry, anger, and this new kind of terror that I couldn't describe.

The intern must have seen the look on my face change because he tried to scramble in front of Annie.

Not the brightest move.

"What in the name of everything were you thinking? How could you possibly come here alone and think that you would be able to survive if something was here?" I demanded.

Then, as they both opened their mouths to speak, I yelled at them again. "NO! No! No, I don't want to hear it. No matter what excuse you have, it's not good enough to justify this kind of action. I swear, if the two of you were part of my command, I would shoot you out of a rekking airlock for your stupidity. AHH!"

I got to my feet, untangled myself from my gear, and marched over to them. I stared the intern down, not difficult ,since he looked like the type of person that would do whatever you wanted in order for you to like him, and brought my voice down to just over a whisper filled with ice.

"You, my moronic student idiot...you will quickly gather together all the gear, place it neatly in my shuttle, and then take the shuttle you two arrived in and return it. Do you understand?"

I never knew a human could nod their head that fast. I thought he was going to shake his own head off.

"Go," I said quietly. He extricated himself from Annie and rushed to do exactly as he was told. Meanwhile, I helped Annie out of her harness and checked her quickly for injuries.

"I'm okay," she insisted as I did a quick field exam, but I wasn't listening. I continued to look her over and, satisfied that nothing was broken, missing, or bleeding, I stepped back and looked at her.

"Are you okay?" I asked, wanting nothing more than to wrap her in my arms, refuse to let her go. "Really?"

She nodded. "Just scared. And a little freaked out."

She watched as the intern raced through packing everything up, placing it in my shuttle. He moved faster than I would've thought possible and before long, he was in the air and flying away.

"What were you thinking?" I asked, back under control.

Barely.

She turned to look at me, chin up, ready for a fight.

"I wanted to get more information. I was trying to help."

"You can't just do something like that without me. What if I hadn't gotten here in time? What if those..." I stopped.

Annie looked at me, her face as perplexed as my mind. I couldn't remember what had attacked her. I just knew she had been in the hole, then we were up here.

"I...I..." I stuttered.

"What is it? What's wrong?" she asked.

"What attacked you down there?" I asked her.

She looked at me, then at the crater, then me again.

"I...I don't remember. I remember going down for samples, then something grabbed me. You were there, then we were up here."

"That's what I remember. And that's all." As we stared at one another, each lost for words, my mind could only think of one question.

What did we just fight?

ANNIE

Karzin climbed into the transport unit and powered it up. I could practically feel the rage pouring off his body as he sat next to me.

We flew over the desert in a tense silence. It was unbearable.

"If you want to yell at me some more, you can," I said quietly.

"I want to, but what's the point?" Karzin snapped.

"It might make you feel better," I shrugged.

Karzin fixed me with a piercing glare.

"Make me feel better?" His lip curled up in a snarl. "You know what would make me feel better? Knowing that you aren't going to do something stupid and dangerous every time I turn my back!"

"I'm sorry I came out here alone," I said. "I know it was a stupid idea. I know I don't have the field experience to handle something like this."

"It's not about your field experience!" Karzin snapped. "Why didn't you wait for me? I would've gone down there and collected samples for you."

"That's exactly why I didn't want you to come," I replied. "The last thing I wanted was for you to risk your neck again."

"Your logic is flawed, even for a human," Karzin groaned with frustration.

"General Rouhr sent you to Einhiv without me. I couldn't just sit idly and wait around for someone else to tell me what to do. The moment General Rouhr said Einhiv had been attacked, I knew more people had died. I thought that if I flew out here and collected a few more samples from farther down, I might have a chance at figuring out what's doing this to people."

My thoughts doubled back and my words tumbled over each other as I tried to explain my reasoning. "I was running and hiding through the entire Xathi invasion. I'm not prepared to do that again, not when I might have the power to do something about it."

Karzin let out a heavy sigh before guiding the transport unit back down to the ground. I looked around at our surroundings. We were close to Nyheim now, the forest was thick around us. I didn't see any signs of civilization, though. We must've landed right between settlements.

"Why are we landing here?" I asked.

"I did not want to get distracted by our...discussion," he answered.

"Too angry to fly and fight?"

He stared straight ahead. "I understand that feeling of uselessness. I probably understand it better than you do." His condescending tone irked me, but I stayed silent. I wanted to mend the rift between us, not widen it. Besides, he was right. I saw how helpless he felt when he searched for his family back on the *Aurora*. "But that does not give you the right to put yourself at risk like that. You don't get to do whatever you want in the name of your cause."

"That's exactly what you were doing when you refused to leave the *Aurora*!" I snapped before I could stop myself. "I admit that what I did wasn't a smart idea. I'm sorry that I scared you, I'm sorry that I almost got you killed, but that does not mean you can act like a hypocrite."

"That's different," Karzin said. "I wasn't risking my life or anyone else's on the *Aurora*."

"I'm sorry!" I exclaimed again. "How many more times do you need me to say it? What more do you need me to do to prove to you that I'm sorry? Do you want me to throw out the samples? Will that make us even?"

"Of course not," Karzin scoffed and looked away.

"Then what?" I snapped. "I'm sorry! I'll say it a hundred more times if you need me to. I'm sorry I went to the crater without you. I'm sorry that I didn't want to put you at risk on my behalf."

"You should've let me," Karzin replied. "I should've been down there with you." He gripped the steering mechanism so hard that his knuckles went pale. I feared he would snap it in two if he didn't loosen his grip.

"Why does this bother you so much?" I asked. "Is it because you had to rescue me?"

"No," Karzin said through clenched teeth. "I'm happy I was there to rescue you."

"Could've fooled me," I sighed.

"I'm angry because I've never felt fear like that before." His answer caught me by surprise.

"What?"

"Knowing you were down there alone, hearing you scream, knowing how much pain you were in, was one of the worst experiences of my life. As I dove into the crater, I was consumed with fear that I wouldn't get to you soon enough. That you would slip right through my fingers and be lost to me forever."

His voice was quiet now, almost a whisper.

Something inside me softened. I reached out and placed my hand on his arm.

"When that thing wrapped around my ankle, the only thing I could think of was that I'd never see you again," I murmured.

Karzin turned to look at me, his brow furrowed and anxious. "Annie, I have feelings for you. Serious ones." I felt my heart skip a beat. "And somehow all it means is I'm afraid, knowing that thing can pop up at any moment and take you from me forever."

My breath caught in my chest as I tried to speak. "I feel the same way about you, Karzin," I whispered. "Whenever I don't know what to do, or if I feel afraid, I think about you. When I want to laugh, I think about you. You're the first thing I think about in the morning."

Karzin twisted in his seat to face me. I did the same. "Don't ever do anything like that again. Understood?"

"I won't. I promise." I nodded vigorously.

"Good," he sighed. "Now, come here so I can kiss you."

I leaned across the seat and let him cup my face in his hands and bring my lips to his. He kissed me so passionately that if he hadn't been holding me to him, the sheer force of it would've knocked me back into my seat.

I grabbed at his shirt to pull myself closer, but the

center console was in the way. Karzin pulled away long enough to grab my hips and gently pull me across the console and into his lap. He pulled me in for another kiss. I opened my mouth, tasting his tongue.

My blood began to thrum in my veins as my breath quickened.

"I was so scared I'd never see you again," I whispered between kisses.

"You never need to be scared of that," Karzin assured me. He planted a trail of hot kisses down my neck that made my body tingle all over. I ran my hands along his chest, arms, shoulders, and back, marveling over the smooth planes and sculpted muscles of his body. I wanted to feel more.

I shifted so I could press my body closer to his. I felt something hard press against my thigh. I looked into Karzin's eyes with a wicked grin, before taking my hand and pressing it against the stiffness in his trousers. Karzin let out a groan as his hands snaked up my shirt.

"I've had dreams like this," he chuckled.

"This is better than a dream." I gently nibbled his ear, watching the goosebumps appear on his skin. With a snarl, he lifted my shirt over my head and practically tore my tank off. My breasts were exposed to him and he immediately began kissing and caressing them, which made me shudder with pleasure.

"Let me take you," he growled in my ear. "I need you, need to feel all of you. Now."

My words caught in my throat, I could only nod. The transport unit was small, with a low ceiling. Not at all an ideal location, but waiting until we returned to the *Aurora* felt unbearable.

He turned me until I sat in his lap with my back against his chest. He pushed the waistband of my pants down until they were out of the way. His thick fingers stroked between my thighs, closer and closer to my wet folds, making me writhe in his arms. I lifted my body as much as I could, grabbing onto anything within reach to help me support myself.

He teased me until I was panting. My breath was ragged when I felt one of his fingers inside my pussy.

"Karzin..." I trailed off as another finger went in, stimulating me. I bit his ear and his fingers began to thrust in and out.

"Fuck," I moaned.

"Let yourself go, Annie," he growled.

His fingers drove harder, grinding into me, demanding a response.

I bit my lip as my pussy clenched around his fingers and I came.

Hard.

My vision clouded as wave after wave of pleasure rolled through me.

Behind me, Karzin undid the top of his trousers and positioned himself against me.

In this position, I couldn't see his cock, but I felt every inch as he slowly pulled me down. Every bulge, every ridge hit against my sensitized clit as he stretched me, filling me completely.

Slowly, he guided me down until he was seated deep inside me. I shuddered at the sensation of him. He nipped and licked at the curve of my neck as, with one hand, he caressed my breasts, with the other lifting me at the hip, pulling me back down harder with each thrust.

The windows of the transport unit fogged as our breathing grew heavy and ragged. I leaned back against him, twisting my neck to bring his mouth to mine and kissing him deeply while he thrust into me again and again. His hand left my breasts and traveled down to play between my thighs. I arched my back, crying out in pleasure that was so intense stars appeared behind my eyelids.

Something deep in my core exploded, consuming all of my senses. He held me against him as he sunk deeper inside me, his breath hot in my ear. With a final thrust, I felt him reach his own height of pleasure.

I gripped a metal rung above me to keep myself upright as my muscles turned to jelly. Karzin wrapped his arms around me, holding me to him and kissing my back and shoulders.

"Are you still angry with me?" I asked, breathless and unable to stop smiling.

Karzin's laugh reverberated through me.

"If this is how we solve our problems, I think we should fight every day."

KARZIN

"I don't know what to do with you," General Rouhr said as I sat in his office. "While you did right in rescuing Annie, you abandoned your assignment in Einhiv."

"My sincerest apologies for disobeying your orders, sir, but I made a judgment call with the knowledge that the situation in Einhiv was handled."

He was right, however. I had disobeyed orders and abandoned my post. Although, if I had not abandoned my post, Annie would surely be dead, and we would have absolutely no information about anything.

"I've always wondered what kind of general I would be, what kind of leader would I turn myself into to make sure I got the best out of my people." He got up from his chair, walked over to a nearby cabinet, and pulled out two glasses and a bottle. He poured the dark amber-colored liquid about one-third of the way in each glass, put the stopper back in the bottle, and brought the glasses back to his desk, setting one in front of me. "I've been a military man for far too long, yet I've never been a stickler for the rules if my people could justify their actions. What you did? That was smart. You made the right decision, and I commend you for that."

I was confused. "Then, if you don't mind the question, why are you reprimanding me?"

"Who said I was reprimanding you?" He took a drink. "I was simply asking what I should do with you. Karzin, I know that you've been struggling lately, and I know that you're angry with us for not making a priority of finding a way home. I'm not happy with it either. I'm really not." He leaned forward on his desk, hands clasped in front of him. "I know you never wanted to be part of this work because it pulled you away from your search, but I needed the real Karzin back."

Ah. This wasn't a reprimand, this was Rouhr being a leader. "I understand that, sir, and...thank you."

"For what?"

It was my turn to take a drink. It was good, smooth. The humans knew their alcohol. "For pulling me out of my own head. For making me realize that what I was doing was more harmful than helpful."

"Well, about that. Your satellite scanning grid is fantastic." I was a bit surprised. How did he know? "Fen filled me in on your search patterns and style and, while I'm not happy with how much it consumed you and changed you, I am impressed with how much space you've charted. Fen tells me that if and when we get back into space, we'll have a highly detailed map to start with."

That's how he knew. I should have figured Rouhr and Fen were in contact with one another. "Thank you, sir. In my obsession, I didn't want to leave anything overlooked. I may have taken things a bit far in the process."

Rouhr finished his drink, raised his eyebrow to ask if I wanted another and, when I shook my head, he nodded and put his own glass away. "You've changed, my friend. You're not the same man you were a year ago."

"Neither are you, if you don't mind my saying."

He laughed, a nice hearty laugh. "That is probably the most obvious statement either of us could have made. Who would have thought that we would end up on a mysterious planet and make friends with the people that lived there?"

"Not just friends, look at you and Team One."

"Very true," he said with a knowing nod. "And to think, not only has Team One found women to love that aren't of their species, but one of them is about to become a father!"

"Yeah. I never had Vrehx down as the fatherly type. He was more military than you," I chuckled.

"Well, that's not hard to do." He then looked at me with a face that made no sense to me. "What about you?"

"Sir?"

"What about you?" He repeated, emphasizing each word. "You left your post to go chasing after a gut feeling about Annie. Would you have done that if she meant nothing to you?"

And there it was.

The idea that I, much like Team One and the general himself, had fallen in love with a human woman. I had never thought it possible. I wasn't a xenophobe, I had many friends amongst the other races.

I just never imagined that I would love anyone other than a Valorni woman. I had spent my entire life fully believing that any woman that wasn't Valorni wasn't worth my effort.

I had come to despise the human women for what they had done to Team One because of that belief. They were fantastic women, and much more capable than I had given them credit for. I respected them greatly, but they had ruined the men, according to my alcohol- and grief-addled mind.

Then I was forced to guard Annie, and when I insulted her, she shot back and defended herself. It was that moment that snapped something inside me. I didn't hate her. I didn't despise her. I wasn't even angry anymore. I acted angry because it was easy for me. It had become habit, but I really wasn't.

It was because of her that I had started to get out of my head and back into reality. Unfortunately, or fortunately depending on how you decided to view it, that reality included living here and most likely never finding my way home. But what if I could make a home here, with Annie? Would I be pleased with that?

"I would like to believe so, sir, but if I was honest with myself, no, I would not have. I would have finished everything in Einhiv and come back here."

"So, she means something to you?" he asked.

I nodded. "Yes, sir. She does. She…I'll never give up trying to find a way off of Ankou and back to Valorn, back to the fight with the Xathi. They are a danger too worrisome to forget."

"That they are."

"But Annie has helped me realize that what the rest of you have, I now want for myself. This is home, for now. Maybe for the rest of our lives, and I need to accept that." The conversation soon shifted to what had happened in the crater. I still couldn't remember exactly what it was, but I knew that we had been attacked.

I just couldn't remember what attacked us.

I soon left his office and decided to walk around the city. The parts of Nyheim that had not been destroyed by the Xathi were beautiful, and the residents had done a good job putting it back into shape.

The part that made me most proud was that they hadn't tried to hide from the destruction of the original crash site. The half of Nyheim that lay in ruins was open for all to see, and was now used to try to rebuild, or build anew.

That got me to thinking about Annie and her family and the way they lived. Their house was far too small and cramped, but with Annie the only one working, it was the best they could get.

There were still good homes here, homes big enough for a family of five, maybe six. There were buildings that, if properly repaired and renovated, would make superb boarding houses for someone like Finola.

Thinking of Finola, I called her up.

"Mr. Karzin!" she exclaimed.

"I wanted to see how your new leg was working," I said to her.

"I couldn't imagine that I'd ever get a new lease on life, but you've given me one, Mr. Karzin," she gushed.

"I am glad."

"Please be more than glad," she continued. "Please know you've given me hope."

"It was the least I could do after your kindness."

"It was you who was kind, Mr. Karzin. Your assistance around the boarding house helped more than you will know."

"I'll still keep a room there, even though I haven't been there for a while," I told her.

"I have half a mind not to charge you."

"I insist."

There was a pause.

Finally, with what I could assume was a smile, she said, "You're a good man, Mr. Karzin. I am sincerely glad to have met you."

Finola was a strong woman, and hearing that she was doing better made me smile.

Staying on this planet might be a good thing. As I walked, I found myself in a neighborhood still under reconstruction. Not many of the homes were being worked on, and several of the homes looked structurally sound enough to live in. I decided to look into one.

"Can I help you?"

I turned around. An old man, older than Vidia, was

standing in the doorway of the home I had entered. "My apologies, sir. I didn't know the home was occupied. I was thinking of getting a dwelling within the city."

"Well, in that case, my own apologies for startling you. I don't exactly own this place, but I'm trying to take care of it for the people that do…or did. I'm still not sure if they're alive."

"I'm sorry, sir. I truly am." I suddenly had a wild idea. "Is there a home around here that you know for certain is vacant?"

Maybe there was something else I could do.

ANNIE

Leena was already waiting for me when I returned to the *Aurora's* lab. I placed my bag on the counter and started unpacking the wealth of samples I'd collected.

Leena's eyes widened with glee when she realized the size of the bounty I'd brought in.

"We have so much to work with!" she gushed. "How did you get this much?"

"Haven't you heard?" I asked. "I threw myself into a bottomless crater in the middle of a desert and almost died."

"Wow. You've earned some respect in my book, for sure," Leena laughed.

"If only Karzin reacted that way," I snorted.

"He was angry?" Leena asked.

"I didn't tell him I was going to throw myself into a crater," I winced." Needless to say, he was a bit put out when he had to rescue me."

"Rescue?" Leena blinked. "Did something go wrong?"

"I may or may not have been attacked by whatever's been leaving the organic traces in the soil," I shrugged. I didn't expect Leena to burst out laughing, but she did.

"Is it bad that I'm jealous?" she asked.

"Yes!" I exclaimed. "I've got scrapes and bruises all up one of my legs. If Karzin hadn't shown up when he did, I would've found out firsthand whether or not the crater has a bottom."

"You also would've found out what grabbed your leg. How exciting would that have been?" Leena's eyes gleamed.

"You're a little scary, you know that?" I asked.

"I've been told," Leena nodded. "I'm used to high stakes when it comes to work. Now that the Xathi are gone, there hasn't been much for me to do. I don't like being idle."

"So, a crater monster is a blessing for you," I joked.

"I wouldn't go that far," Leena amended. "Entirely."

"I'm starting to see why you and Axtin get on so well," I replied. "I've never met him, but if he's anything like Karzin, I'd say you two are well matched."

"Thanks." Leena's smile softened. "I think we're well

matched, too. You remind me of myself in some ways, which would explain why Karzin is so taken with you."

"Really?" I stammered. Of course, Karzin and I were taken with each other, but I didn't know how Leena knew about that.

"It's obvious!" Leena exclaimed. "Karzin was unreachable for months. You show up and suddenly he's going above and beyond. Whatever you're doing with him, it's working."

"He's very special," I smiled more to myself than to Leena. "It makes me happy to remind him of that fact."

"That's disgustingly sweet," Leena laughed. "All right. Enough sappy stuff. Let's get to the samples."

"Right." I'd almost forgotten why I was here. When I thought about Karzin, everything else went out the window.

Leena and I started with the largest sample taken from the deepest point in the crater.

"How far down were these collected?" she asked.

"I don't know," I groaned. "I was down there by myself and the intern didn't measure the rope. And, of course, I don't remember."

"Shoddy fieldwork,' she clicked her tongue as she prepared the sample for analysis.

"Rappel alone into an endless void, then you can judge me," I replied.

"Fair enough," Leena shrugged. "We should be

grateful any of the samples survived at all after that thing grabbed you."

The *Aurora* analyzed the sample quickly. When the results appeared on the console, Leena gave a surprised gasp.

"Interesting," she murmured. "This is a variant of the toxin that leaked from the Xathi ship fragments."

"How did it get down that deep?" I wondered.

"It has corrosive properties." Leena pointed to the console. "This chemical compound here is highly acidic."

"This part here looks familiar." I pointed to part of the analysis of the organic material. The *Aurora's* lab was able to generate a genetic analysis of the organic sample.

"It looks similar to the genomes of the sentient plant species. They all have a few common traits," Leena explained.

"The toxic substance was found with the organic material. It's fair to say they likely came in contact with each other."

"Let me run a simulation of that reaction. I have enough data to generate one." Leena typed a few things into the console. "We have the chemical makeup of the toxic substance and the makeup of the organic material. We don't have exact amounts and we don't know how long they were exposed to each other."

"At most, two months," I replied. "That's when the Xathi ship fragments crashed back down."

"I'll put that in and see what happens."

Leena ran the simulation. The toxic substance overpowered the organic material, degrading it.

"It reminds me of the reaction that occurs when human skin is exposed to acid," Leena replied.

"That can't feel good," I frowned.

"That's assuming whatever is down there can feel," Leena interjected.

"Would now be a good time to call that woman you told me about?" I asked. "Jeneva, her name was?"

"Vrchx won't be happy, but I think she's the only person on this planet who can tell us more," Leena sighed. She pulled out a comm unit.

"Hello?" A woman's voice answered on the other end of the line.

"Jeneva, it's Leena. I've got a favor to ask of you," Leena said.

"I've been placed on leave for the duration of my pregnancy," Jeneva grumbled. "I'm not supposed to do anything."

"I've got samples of an unidentified organic material that shares traits with sentient plants," Leena said in a sing-song voice.

"I'll be there in ten minutes." Jeneva disconnected.

"Maternity leave for her entire pregnancy?" I asked. "That seems extreme. Is she unwell?"

"No, she's fine. It's just the first time a human female has carried the child of a Skotan male, so everyone is treating her like blown glass," Leena explained.

"She's pregnant with an alien's baby?" I couldn't hide my surprise. "I didn't even know that was possible."

"Neither did anyone else," Leena laughed dryly.

True to her word, Jeneva arrived at the lab in record time. She was taller than I'd expected her to be, and willowy thin, despite her pregnant state. She wasn't far along by the look of it, but far along enough to have a sizable baby bump.

Jeneva and Leena greeted each other with a hug.

"You're positively glowing," Leena beamed.

"I don't feel like it," Jeneva laughed. "I've never been so tired and hungry in all of my life, even though all I do now is eat and sleep."

"Does Vrehx know you're here?" Leena asked.

"He does," Jeneva nodded. "He's been a nervous wreck ever since he found out I'm pregnant. It's cute."

"I can't imagine Vrehx nervous," Leena chuckled.

"Teasing him about it is my greatest source of entertainment," Jeneva said with a wicked grin. I tried not to stare, but I couldn't take my eyes off her. She was a walking miracle.

I had every intention of staying with Karzin forever,

but I'd always assumed children were out of the question. I hadn't given much thought to children in general, human or otherwise.

Now that I looked at Jeneva and saw how happy and settled she was, I couldn't help but feel a little jealous. I realized I wanted what she had. Hopefully, Karzin felt the same way.

But that was a conversation for another time. Jeneva wasn't here just so I could gawk at her.

"I'm Annie Parker. Geologist," I stuck out my hand. Jeneva shook it.

"I hear you've found something out in the desert," she smiled. "I'll be happy to take a look. I love being waited on hand and foot all day, but I miss my work."

I showed Jeneva our data, specifically the genetic profile pulled from the organic material.

"Interesting," Jeneva muttered as she peered closer.

"Jeneva's made a name for herself in the plant field," Leena explained.

"The more technical aspects of all this," Jeneva waved at the lab, "I've come to pretty recently. I used to live in the forest," she continued. "I made a living harvesting poison, sap, and extracts from plants and animals. Not a lot of exact science, but always interesting."

"That sounds like a terrifying job," I replied.

"It had its moments," Jeneva admitted. "But I didn't

have a choice. At the time, living in the city wasn't an option."

"Why not?" I asked. I immediately chided myself for asking such personal questions.

"You don't need to feel bad. I don't mind answering questions about my life," Jeneva said.

I blinked in surprise, wondering if I'd voiced my thoughts. "I'm an empath. I can read other people's feelings, emotions, and occasionally their thoughts."

"That's incredible," I stammered.

Jeneva was, officially, the most interesting person on Ankou.

"It was horrible at first. My husband, Vrehx, was the one who taught me how to control it. It's thanks to him that I get to have a life," she beamed.

"Any progress on identifying the plant, Jeneva? I've got something strange over here," Leena said, drawing focus back to the issue at hand.

"Whatever it is, it belongs to the same family as the other sentient plants, but the similarities stop there. I have no idea what it is," Jeneva sighed. "What have you got?"

"Traces of an airborne substance trapped in the soil," Leena said. "I shifted the sample just a little. I must've released the gas without realizing it."

"What sample is it from?" I asked. Leena checked the label.

"It's from Malvor. I'm going to run a few tests." Leena quickly became absorbed in her task. Once again, I was amazed at the efficiency of the *Aurora's* lab. Leena had results in minutes.

"I don't understand," she muttered to the console.

"What is it?" Jeneva and I asked at the same time.

"This gas, whatever it is, causes memory loss," she said, pulling up data from her pad. "I've run some initial samples through and it looks like the gas contains molecules that interfere in brain chemistry in humans. The most noticeable side effect is that it prevents memory formation."

"That explains why no one remembers the attacks," I sighed.

"I'll get working on an antidote," Leena sighed. "No promises it'll work."

"That's all we can ask for at this point."

KARZIN

I waited for Annie outside the *Aurora's* lab.

When she left the lab and saw me waiting for her in the corridor, her whole face lit up with the most stunning smile.

"What are you doing here?" she asked.

"Taking you out to dinner," I replied. "I planned ahead and made sure the restaurant had a table available, so you can't turn me down."

Annie gasped and looked down at her wrinkled, dirt-stained clothes. "I can't go to dinner! All my clothes look like this," she exclaimed.

At that moment, Leena breezed by with a wry smile.

"The dress you asked me to bring is hanging in Annie's room, Karzin," she informed me.

"You knew about this?" Annie asked.

"Of course," Leena said with a dismissive wave of her hand. "Don't spill anything on that dress. It's my favorite."

"Thank you, Leena." I bowed to her as she walked away.

"You really put effort into planning this," Annie laughed.

"Yes, I did. Now go get dressed." I winked at her as she hurried off to her borrowed room.

When she reappeared twenty minutes later, she was completely transformed. Her skin glowed under the ship's overhead lights. The dress Leena lent was simple and black, but hugged every curve of Annie's perfect body. She wore black strappy things on her feet that looked like beautiful instruments of torture. Her hair shone like polished copper.

"You look amazing." I felt breathless. "You're going to make me look bad." In those shoes, she was several inches taller. Tall enough to plant a kiss on my cheek without straining upward.

"Impossible," she smiled up at me. I offered her my arm and asked Fen to open a rift for us. When we stepped off the *Aurora,* Annie's expression tightened but she didn't hesitate to step through the rift into the heart of Nyheim.

"You didn't even flinch that time!" I praised, rubbing her bare arms with my hands to warm her up.

"I still hate it," she laughed. "It's a shame it's so convenient."

There was only one proper restaurant operating in Nyheim. The city had rebuilt itself just enough so that such luxuries were available, but only sparingly.

No matter the universe, formal rituals for dining seemed to serve the same purposes.

Despite everything, people wanted a sense of normalcy. A place to go to celebrate their triumphs and spend time with their loved ones.

It wasn't the prettiest place, but I didn't think Annie would mind. Inside, the concrete walls were punctuated by exposed pipes. Whoever owned the place had tried to make the pipes look better by wrapping them in strings of tiny lights.

Annie couldn't stop looking around, her mouth opened in delight. The restaurant could have been made of rubble for all I cared. All I wanted to see was her.

A pleasant woman led us to a quiet table in the back. A single lit candle was placed in the center of the table.

"This is lovely," Annie beamed as she took her seat.

"I'm glad you like it."

"Thank you for bringing me here." Annie looked soft and pretty in the candlelight. I wanted to touch her, but somehow refrained.

"Did you have a productive day with Leena?" I asked.

"I did," she smiled. "We figured out why no one can remember the attacks."

I perked up with interest. "Why?"

"It's an unknown species of sentient plant with the ability to produce a gas that affects memory formation," I explained.

"That's insane." I shook my head. Just when I thought this planet couldn't get any stranger. "If that's the case, how come we remember being attacked?"

"I actually have a theory on that," Annie said between bites of soft, buttery bread. "I think the attacks are planned in advance. When we went into the crater, we caught the creature-thing by surprise, so it didn't have time to excrete enough of the gas to completely wipe our memories." She licked her lips, and my gut clenched. "Either that, or it has a limited supply of the gas, and had exhausted itself with the attack on Einhiv."

"That makes as much sense as everything else that's happened." I chuckled, forcing my thoughts away from her lips. There was something else I wanted to talk about tonight.

"Leena's going to try to make something to block the effects of the gas," she continued, "but it will only work if it's given to people right before an attack."

"We have no way to predict that." I frowned.

"Yet." She looked at me with a gleam in her eyes. "I have faith that you'll come up with an excellent plan of defense." She reached across the table to grab both of my hands.

"Let's not talk about work anymore." I smiled. "I brought you here because there's something I need to tell you."

"Oh?" Annie's expression brightened. "Should I be worried?"

"We'll see," I joked.

I felt nervous, a sensation I wasn't overly familiar with. Funny, I could face down a Xathi hoard without batting an eye, yet this small human female constantly unsettled me. "I brought you here to thank you."

"Thank me?" She blinked in surprise, caught off guard.

"Yes. I've been hiding for the last two months. Yes, I've been searching for my family, but I was using that as an excuse to completely shut myself away from the world. It wasn't right. I'm going to continue to search for my family, but I don't want to shut myself away anymore. I want to move forward and have a real life. I wouldn't want that if it weren't for you," I told her.

"You would've pulled yourself out of your dark place eventually," she said demurely.

"Maybe." I shrugged. "But it would've taken much longer. You brought me back to life. I'm ready to stop living in the past. I want to live in the moment and I want you by my side."

"I'd be honored to stand by you," she grinned. The nerves dissipated as she smiled at me. I felt invincible.

"I found a place in Nyheim. It's close to where I work, it's close to where you work. I want you to live there with me." Her face lit up for an instant before sadness tinged her expression.

"There's nothing I want more," she said. "But my family is completely dependent on me. I can't leave them."

"I've thought of that," I grinned. I reached into my pocket and pulled out a datapad displaying the ad for the second home, a three-bedroom house on the outskirts of Nyheim. "It's not much to look at, but it has plenty of space."

"My family can't afford a place like that," she said, shaking her head.

"I've already bought both," I blurted, then held my breath.

Annie made a strange choking noise as she looked at me, wide-eyed.

"How wealthy are you?"

I leaned back and laughed. This I could deal with. "One of the first things that General Rouhr did after the war was to negotiate with the human leaders for an exchange rate between Alliance currency and your credit system. Since we can't exactly transfer credits from home, we're trading by upgrading the power systems, using the technology from the Urai and the K'ver."

"Okay," Annie said, not grasping.

"Take into account the back pay that all the soldiers on the *The Vengeance* had accumulated. Hazard pay. Combat pay. All of it."

Her eyes narrowed. "So, you're rich?"

"Not exactly, but enough that it let me buy both houses and give your parents one to live in while we live in the other," I finished.

"You can't be serious," she gasped. Her eyes filled with tears.

"I am," I assured her. "I've saved nearly all of my wages. I have more than enough to live comfortably. If I can't help my own family right now, please let me help yours."

"I don't know what to say." A tear slipped down her cheek.

I reached across the table to wipe it away. "Say yes," I urged.

"Yes!" she laughed, then stood up from her seat and walked around to embrace me. I held her close until she pulled away. "Can I see our new home?"

"Now?" I asked. "We haven't ordered."

"Now," she nodded. "There's something I want to do

that's better than dinner." The mischievous gleam in her eyes told me everything I needed to know.

I stood up from the table, took her hand and left, apologizing to the very nice hostess on the way out.

Annie giggled the entire way, her steps hampered by the shoes until I swept her up into my arms. "We don't own any furnishings yet," I warned her.

"That's okay! I just want to see it," she laughed. Annie burst into the house before me. The main room was spacious. There was also a kitchen filled with appliances I didn't understand, two washrooms, and several bedrooms.

"It's perfect!" she beamed. She turned back to face me. "You're perfect."

I closed the door behind me. "Come here," I instructed. I opened my arms for her, catching her as she ran to me. I tipped her head up with two fingers and bent down to kiss her.

"Will you be happy here?" I asked between kisses.

"I'm happy anywhere as long as you're with me," she replied.

"I never want you to leave my side," I murmured. "I love you, Annie."

"I love you, too, Karzin." I let myself get lost in her kisses, the soft feel of her perfect lips melting into mine like discovering my love for her anew. Slowly, our kisses turned from sweet and soft to rough and filled with heat, her lips parted for my tongue to dance with hers. Desire seared through me, clouding my thoughts.

Annie appeared to feel the same.

"I want you," she whimpered against my mouth.

"Take off your dress," I growled.

She stepped away from me, a playful smile on her perfect lips. With hungry eyes, I watched her shimmy out of the dress. When she moved to take off her shoes, I stopped her.

"Leave those on."

She smiled coyly and returned to my embrace.

I ran my hands over every inch of her silky skin, from the elegant curve of her neck to the swell of her perfect breasts.

Then came my tongue. My mouth claimed every inch of her, from the taut warmth of her stomach to the delicate curves of her hips. I tasted her body, heard her moans as my hands and mouth explored her. I couldn't get enough of her.

"Karzin," Annie said, her breath hitched in her throat. "Please."

"I want you, Annie. I want to savor you."

I meant my words. I brought her breasts to my mouth, tongue sweeping over the hard peaks of her nipples. I took one breast in my mouth, and caressed the other, feeling her roll and writhe under my ministrations. The sight of her breasts wet and glistening from my mouth was glorious. I pulled her tight to me and ran my tongue down the curve of her neck to her collarbone.

Then I trailed my mouth down lower as I pressed my hardness against her so she could feel just how much I wanted her.

"I need to taste you." Kneeling in front of her, I slipped my arms around her legs, pulling her towards me. My tongue teased every sensitive fold and I nuzzled my nose delicately against her pussy. At first, I was gentle, hearing her need growing. I wanted to tantalize her.

Annie moaned, and, in an instant, her fingers laced behind my head as she moved my mouth to please her everywhere she desired it. I wanted her to have total bliss, many times, before I entered her.

Even though I wanted to sheathe myself in her instantly, I knew that if I waited and prepared, it would be best for us both if I brought her to a pinnacle of pleasure. I wanted that for Annie. I wanted her completely, to taste every inch of her. The wetness of her pleasure painted my face.

Circling her clit with my tongue, I slowly slid one finger into her; her wet heat a drug I'd never want to break free from. A second finger joined the first, then a third, as I drove them into her pussy, twisting and pumping until she clutched at my hair, knees shaking.

"Yes!" she whimpered. "I'm coming!"

Those words were magic to my ears as I held her closer, drawing desire from her with all my energy and strength.

Her head fell back and her mouth went slack. Her whole body shivered and shuddered. Moans escaped her lips, half words and sighs as her orgasm coursed through her.

I moaned into her pussy, drinking every last drop of pleasure I could from her as the vibrations of my moans aroused her further. The way she shook in rhythm and reaction to me was deeply sensual, satisfactory on a level I didn't know I could experience until I shared this with her.

I licked up every bit of her honey and savored the shudders of desire that rode through her in waves. "Again." It wasn't just a command. It was a promise. I wanted her to come more, and I wanted to taste that orgasm, too, before I sunk into her.

Her legs were wobbly with need, and I held her up as I pleasured her. "I won't let you fall," I whispered against her quivering pussy. "You taste delicious," I told her, again letting the heat of my words bring more pleasure against her -- hot breath on hot skin.

"I love celebrating with you, Annie." I nibbled against her thigh and breathed against her pussy before my mouth reclaimed it, and I sucked tightly on her clit with a suction that made her surrender.

She writhed against me, moaned, and gripped me tightly as her legs quaked.

She cried out, her body seeming to be out of her control entirely as pleasure was her master. At first, she quivered intensely, and then her body became limp and her moans were lower and quieter.

When I knew the second orgasm had run through her, I stood, gliding my hands up her body, and turned her face up to mine. I captured her lips in a kiss so she could taste herself.

"To our future," I told her when we finally broke our kiss to catch our breaths.

"I want to touch you," she gasped, slim fingers working my shirt open. Happy to help, I unfastened my trousers, kicked my shoes out of the way.

Her hands were gliding across my bare chest, running down my sides, lit flames in their path.

"I wondered about the stripes," she murmured, one hand pressing my aching cock, rubbing until I thought I'd go mad.

"Later," I growled. "Later you can trace all of them. But I have to be in you now, Annie."

I lifted her off the floor, her legs wrapped around my waist.

Once she was in my arms, I lowered myself to the

floor. She giggled and held tight to me, curling against me as I wrapped her in my arms.

The cold of the bare floor was nothing to me. My body was alive where she touched me and the heat between us radiated, matching our joy.

The city lights streamed in from the one window, illuminating her bare skin.

I reached up, cupping her breasts in my hands. I watched goosebumps appear on her skin as I gently caressed her, then rolled her tight nipples between my fingers. She tipped her head back and opened her mouth with a soft moan. Her hips began rocking back and forth against me, and her still-wet pussy ground against my hard cock, every bulge straining against her smooth human body.

Annie rose up, positioning herself until she was directly above me. The sight of her over me, her perfect tits and her wet pussy, made my cock even harder.

I lifted my hips to tease her entrance, erasing the space between us and pressing myself against her wet folds, running the thick head of my cock over her as she painted me with her desire.

From our heated joining in the transport unit, I knew she'd be able to take me.

And this was better. I could watch her face as she gasped and shuddered, shivering as she slowly lowered herself and took every inch of me, neither of us able to wait or tease even a moment longer.

The way her eyes rolled up in her head and she bit her lower lip, her face a mask of ultimate desire, I knew that we weren't just functionally compatible. We were experiencing bliss as we joined together.

Air hissed through my teeth as she enveloped me in her soft, slick pussy.

I gripped her hips, guiding her motions as she moved herself up and down, grinding against her with every thrust. The smoothness of her velvet vise gripping my cock was perfection.

I claimed and marked her.

Made her mine.

Eyes wide, she placed a hand on my chest to steady herself. I moved one hand back to her breasts, kneading the soft globes, teasing every nerve of her skin.

"You look beautiful in the lights." I looked into her eyes. "In our home."

I watched, mesmerized, as she rocked her body against mine, swallowing every inch of me with her tight pussy. As she rode me, every ridge manipulated her delicate pussy walls until she quaked, shivering in delight.

"Karzin," she moaned my name in a breathy voice.

Hearing her whisper my name was my undoing.

I gripped her hips, holding her in place as I thrust up

into her, faster and faster with each stroke, my cock needing to claim her even harder. Faster.

I felt her tighten around me. Incredible heat surged from her, and her grip was a thundering heartbeat of lust.

Her legs began to tremble as unrestrained cries of pleasure tore from her lips.

As she screamed, I held her to me, shuddering as I found the heights of my pleasure with her, my cock erupting as I filled her with my seed. “My Annie.” My perfect Annie.

She went limp on my chest as she gasped, catching her breath. I held her close to me, shielding her from the chill of the cold floor.

Claiming her because I needed her to still be in my arms.

I would always hold her, house her, protect her.

Annie was mine.

Would always be mine.

Just the thought made my cock twitch again.

Annie felt it and gave a soft moan, enough to make me harden again. But for now, I was content to just hold her.

Breathe in her scent.

“I love you so much.” The words couldn’t be denied. She deserved the truth. Deserved everything.

Her soft breasts pressed to the hard wall of my

chest. “Karzin, I love you more than I even knew I could.”

The raw emotion in her voice touched me deep inside.

“Let’s stay like this for a while.” I kissed the top of her head, caressing her back, memorizing every soft curve.

We lay there together for hours, whispering sweet nothings to each other in the dark until the light of day shone through the window of our new home.

Home. With my mate.

ANNIE

"You look nervous." Karzin gave me a gentle nudge as we rode the elevator up to General Rouhr's office.

"I *am* nervous." I forced a laugh, but I felt like I was going to throw up.

"Don't be!" Karzin encouraged. "Although, you probably should've gotten more sleep last night."

"And who's fault is that?" I exclaimed.

While Karzin and I scrounged for furniture for our new place, I spent most of my nights on the *Aurora*. Sleeping was rarely a priority in his cabin.

"Yours, for being so easily seduced by a handsome Valorni," Karzin teased.

I swatted his arm.

The elevator door opened and we made our way to

General Rouhr's office. He'd gathered the members of Strike Teams One, Two, and Three in a large conference room. Councilwoman Vidia was there, as well. I don't know why, but I'd always had the impression that she'd look older. I quickly noticed the affectionate gazes she traded with General Rouhr.

"Are they together?" I whispered to Karzin.

"Yes. It surprised all of us. We never thought Rouhr would slow down enough to find a mate," he explained.

"Good for them," I nodded.

I spotted Jeneva sitting in a cushy chair with a hand resting affectionately on her growing belly. A Skotan that had to be Vrehx stood behind her, his red hands resting on her narrow shoulders. Jeneva looked happy, serene, and curious. Vrehx looked the opposite.

Leena was there as well, standing in the back of the room next to a towering Valorni that had to be Axtin. Leena twisted her mouth with impatience. Axtin looked rather bored. I spotted Dr. Parr as well, hand in hand with a Skotan. I hadn't realized she had an alien mate. Apparently, I'd joined a club.

"Sucks to be a human male nowadays," I joked quietly to Karzin. "How could they compete with you and the others."

"They can't," he said with a cocky wink. I rolled my eyes, then took a deep breath to calm my racing heart and looked over the notes on my datapad for the hundredth time.

I had spent the better part of the last three days barricaded in the *Aurora's* lab going over absolutely everything. I wanted to do this right.

"Looks like everyone's here." General Rouhr's deep voice startled me. "I won't take up time with introductions. Annie, if you're ready, we'll start with the information you've gathered." I managed a jerky nod and stood up.

"You're going to do great," Karzin whispered to me as I walked past him. His words helped to settle the knot twisting in my stomach.

General Rouhr gave me a nod of encouragement as he gave me the floor. I stared at the sea of faces watching me. Some looked interested, others looked bored and disinterested.

"H-hello." I cleared my throat. "I'm Annie Parker. I'm a geologist. As you all know by now, human settlements have been targeted by a series of mysterious attacks that have left buildings toppled and people dead. For the last week or so, I've been gathering information in an attempt to identify the mystery assailant. With the help of Dr. Leena Dewitt and Jeneva Calder, we now have an idea of what we're up against."

With each word, I felt my body relax. This wasn't so

bad. I caught Karzin's eye. He smiled at me, pride shining in his eyes.

"From the collected samples, I've been able to determine that the creature attacking the towns and the creature in the crater are the same species. Based on the genetic material salvaged from traces in the soil, it's highly possible that it's a single creature rather than a hive or colony."

Everyone's expression shifted to various degrees of disbelief.

"That would mean this creature, whatever it is, is gigantic!" Axtin exclaimed. I nodded.

"That's correct. With Leena and Jeneva's guidance, I've run tests to determine an approximate age of this creature as well. It could be anywhere from a century old to several thousand years old." Gasps and murmurs broke out amongst the crowd.

"How is that possible?" someone asked.

"This creature belongs to the same family as all of the sentient plants on this planet," I continued. "There have been sorvuc found that are over one hundred years old. I expect the creature we're dealing with possesses the same longevity genes."

"Why is this only being discovered now?" a serious looking K'ver asked.

"I don't know," I sighed. "It's den, if you will, appears to be in that crater out in the desert. When humans originally settled here, they only performed in-depth analysis on the areas that were most habitable. The desert environment wouldn't have been one of those areas."

"Tell me about it," a Valorni from Strike Team One mumbled. It wasn't the one with Leena, so it must be... Daxion. I wondered what he'd found out in the desert.

"Why is the creature stirring now?" Vrehx asked.

"I believe that when the remains of the Xathi ship crashed back down onto the surface of the planet, it weakened the earth beneath it. Several of those fragments contained a toxic substance that sunk into the soil. Dr. Dewitt discovered that the substance essentially dissolved the organic material belonging to the creature in the crater. I suspect that when it came into contact with the toxin, it became irritated. It might've been hibernating at the time, I don't know for certain, but that would explain why we haven't had a problem with it before now."

"Why attack the human settlements, though?" Councilwoman Vidia asked.

"Going on the theory that this creature was in a state of hibernation, it's possible the toxins woke it up and it realized that the only thing in the environment that had changed was the human settlements," I explained. "I can't say why the creature attacked the specific cities that it did. It's possible that it had something to do with soil density. Distance doesn't seem to be a factor."

"And the memory loss?" Sylor asked.

"That's also a product of the creature. It's likely that it can secrete a gas that alters a person's memory," I explained.

"I'm working on something to negate the effects of the gas," Leena spoke up. "However, it's impossible to test without exposing someone to the gas and it will only work if taken before an attack."

"My team and I have been working towards preventive measures," Karzin jumped in. "Our best bet at the moment is mounted cameras under twenty-four-hour surveillance, but until we get a good look at the thing, we don't have much to go on."

"Basically, all we can do is wait until whatever that thing is strikes again?" Axtin asked. "That won't do anyone any good."

"I've reached out to some of my colleagues from university," Leena interjected. "I'm looking for anyone with expertise that might be able to help us. A friend of mine is a well-known botanist. They might be able to tell us more about the creature."

"That's nice, and all," one of the Skotan brothers on Karzin's team spoke up, "but that doesn't solve anything. All we have is a handful of possible facts that won't do much to help anyone if the creature decides to attack again."

"Rokul," Karzin muttered in a warning tone.

"It's all right," I smiled trying to assure him. "Rokul is correct. We hardly have any helpful information."

"I suggest doubling our efforts for emergency response," Rouhr jumped in. "The amount of cameras should be doubled in every city and settlement. We have to perfect our response times. With Fen and the Gateway at our disposal, there's no reason why we can't be on the scene within minutes of an alert going out."

"I think we should allocate efforts to removing the Xathi debris," I added. "If the toxic substance from their ship is what irritated the creature in the first place, we have to clean that up as much as we can."

"If it's anything like a sorvuc, it won't give a damn about our clean-up efforts. We've already pissed it off," Jeneva interjected.

"It's better than doing nothing," I replied heavily. "Who knows? It could be more intelligent than a sorvuc."

"Not likely." Jeneva offered a kind smile.

"I think Annie's right," Rouhr decided. "Cleaning up the mess we made might not help anything, but it certainly won't make it worse. Is there anything else you'd like to add, Annie?"

"You all know as much as I do now," I said.

Rouhr gave me a nod and I returned to my seat.

"Well done, love," Karzin whispered as I settled down beside him.

"I walked into this meeting feeling like I'd done so much to solve this mystery," I whispered back, my voice heavy and weary. "Now I know that I've barely scratched the surface. I didn't learn anything truly useful."

"You're being too hard on yourself." Karzin put his arm around me and rubbed my shoulder. "Without you, we'd never know that we're fighting a giant, ancient plant monster. That's a starting point."

"I hope that botanist Leena requested will be able to find out more than I can," I sighed, letting my head rest on Karzin's shoulder.

Rouhr spent the next hour delegating tasks and outlining several tentative plans of attack. None of them were perfect. There was quite a bit of debate regarding whether a ground team or an aerial team would be more effective in case of another attack.

"An aerial team would be safe from the memory loss gas," Karzin argued.

"A ground team would have more precision," Vrehx replied. "It would be too easy for an aerial strike team to accidentally hit a civilian or cause a building to collapse."

"That's a fair point," Karzin allowed. "But how

effective can a ground team hope to be if they forget what they're fighting the moment they get too close?"

"What about a ground team with gas masks?" Vrehx asked.

"Gas masks would impede us if we were involved in hand-to-hand combat," Karzin posited.

In the end, nothing was decided. We simply didn't have enough information. I couldn't help but feel dejected as Karzin and I walked out of the meeting.

"I'm going back to the *Aurora* to lie down for a little while," I said faintly.

"Of course, love. I'll be there shortly." Karzin pressed a kiss onto my forehead and smiled at me so sweetly that I couldn't help but feel a little brighter inside.

KARZIN

We were moving into our new home. I couldn't believe how much of a process it was. We needed furniture, utensils, dishes, towels, cleaning supplies, tools, paint, drywall, lumber, flooring, carpeting. I got lost on the number of things needed.

Luckily, Councilwoman Vidia knew which businesses still had pre-war inventory, or had been able to salvage items. None of it was a necessity, Rhour reminded me, but another way the civilians could feel like life was getting back to normal.

And not just civilians. All of us.

What I found funny after closer inspection was that the house was in good shape. It only needed a little bit of cosmetic work, according to my view point, but

Annie was excited about making some changes and making the house a home.

Not just any home, but *our* home.

"What do you think of taking down that wall there to make the kitchen bigger?" she asked as we were bringing in a couch.

With a grunt, I set my end of the couch down and looked where she was pointing. "Which wall? That one?"

"No, you weirdo. That one."

"Oh." I shrugged. "I think we could, but why. Isn't the kitchen big enough?"

"Well, yeah, but wouldn't it be nicer if it was bigger? We could have the whole team over here, the family, whoever, and there would be lots of room for them to sit around the table, at the island, wherever they wanted to be." She was pointing out where the table would be, the island, the…wait.

"What's an island? I thought that was a body of land surrounded by water? How do we do that inside a house?"

She looked at me, eyes wide and lips curled inward.

I wasn't sure what the problem was. Especially when she broke out into uncontrollable laughter.

Any time she started to calm down, she would look at me and break out into laughter again.

I finally shook my head and walked out of the

house. There were more things that needed to come inside, and I could wait until she made more sense.

I grabbed a side table and a small stool from the trailer outside and took them inside. Annie was standing at the door, looking slightly ashamed.

"I'm sorry. I didn't mean to upset you," she said as she took the stool from me.

"It's just, I don't understand what was so humorous about my question."

She set the stool down, turned to look at me, and came over to give me a kiss. "I'm sorry. You speak my language so fluently now, I forget that not everything is going to translate. An island, specifically a kitchen island, is sort of like a table with cabinets underneath it."

"Ah," I said. I understood her now. "I know what those are. We just never called them islands, because on Valorn, any island was land. We called it a socan."

"Oh, cool. Hey, could you teach me your language one day? I'd like to be able to speak to you in your native language so you can feel a little more at home."

I was already in love with her, but that was probably the sweetest thing she could have said to me.

I grabbed her, pulled her in, and kissed her deeply. "I love you," I said when we separated.

She looked up at me, her hand on my chest while

her other was on my back. "I love you, too. We still need to get the rest of the stuff in the house."

"And if you two didn't waste all of your time kissing, you would get it done."

We both turned to see Sylor standing in the door, holding a chair. "Where do you want this?" As Annie showed him where to put it, the rest of my team came in carrying some of our things.

"What brought this on?" I asked as I rushed over to help Iq'her with a box that was more bulky than heavy.

He shrugged and pointed with his chin to Sylor. "His idea."

I looked at Sylor, who nodded.

"We sort of figured that the faster you're in your new home," he said, "the faster you're back at work doing what you're supposed to do. So, here we are."

"Besides," Takar cut in, "we were curious as to what sort of home you would choose and wanted to see it before you cut us off again."

The barb hurt a bit, but I deserved it. "I won't cut any of you off again. We're a team, a family, and I won't abandon my family."

"Good. Then you can help this family member carry in that ugly table," Takar said with a smile.

"Hey!" Annie said in mock pain. "I picked that table."

"Well, that explains it then," Sylor cut in.

"Explains what?" Annie asked.

Before Sylor could answer, Iq'her finished his joke. "That you choosing Karzin wasn't a mistake, it's a pattern of bad taste."

He had timed it perfectly.

Annie had started drinking from a bottle of water and spit it out with force at Iq'her's words.

I looked at Iq'her in wonder. He stared at me, as serious as could be for a moment, then broke into a smile as the rest of the team ran from the house to hide their laughter.

I turned around to see Annie in shock.

Annie finally joined in and gave Iq'her a light kiss on the cheek as she passed him by.

"That was incredible," I said, still laughing.

Iq'her and the entire team had finally forgiven me

The team spent the rest of the day helping us move things in, and even helped us start tearing the wall down that Annie wanted gone.

Rokul was curious as to why someone would want to tear down a perfectly good wall, but since it wasn't his house, he didn't care.

Annie wanted it, and that was enough for me.

It was late in the evening when they left.

She snuggled against me on the couch, both of us tired and happy. "Thank you."

"For what?"

"For choosing me. For getting my family a new

home…" she hesitated a bit. "For wanting me to live with you."

I chuckled lightly. "Of course, I wanted you to live with me. Who else is going to clean my mess?"

"AH!" Her jaw dropped and she shot away from me and smacked me on the arm. "What?"

"Well, you want me to clean up my own messes?" I asked playfully.

"You're damn right, mister. And you're going to do dishes, and even the laundry, too," she shot back at me.

I pretended to think about it for a quick moment, and as her eyes squinted more and more, I held up my hands in mock surrender. "Okay, I think I can handle that," I said with a smile.

"You better," she mumbled as she snuggled back up against me. We sat there holding one another for so long I lost track of what time of night it was. We just sat, enjoying being together and listening to music.

After a while, as I felt as though I was falling asleep, Annie spoke up again. "What are we going to do in the backyard?"

"What do you mean?" I asked.

"Well," she pulled away from me and turned so we could look directly at one another. "It's big enough for us to do a lot of things with. I wouldn't mind having a few pets back there and maybe…" she stopped and looked at me.

I saw that she was a bit nervous.

"Maybe what?" I asked.

"Maybe some kids?" she said hesitantly. "I mean, the house and the yard are big enough for a *bunch* of animals and kids. I could see something crazy like a dozen animals or kids playing back there and running around the house. You know…if we were crazy."

Kids.

Children.

With Annie.

That sounded...wonderful.

I could see children playing in the yard, maybe not as many as twenty, but certainly several.

I pulled her back into my lap. "That could be fun. A little miniature Andromeda, with your beautiful hair."

She frowned a bit, nestling into my chest. "As long as it doesn't clash with their green skin."

A flash of worry ran through me.

Vrehx and Jeneva were going to be the first couple with a hybrid child, and everyone was hoping things were going to be fine.

Skotans aren't as big as Valorni.

I looked at Annie and realized that, if she was willing to try to become a mother, I wanted to be the father.

If she was brave enough to rappel into a bottomless

crater, together we could figure it out. And my fears for her safety couldn't run our lives.

"Maybe one of those little hairy things you humans are so fond of. What are they called? Dogs?"

She bounced and nodded "Not a little dog, though. I want a full-size dog when it grows up. A big one," she added.

"Sounds perfect."

It really did.

EPILOGUE: ANNIE

"I'm excited to try the food this time," I murmured to Karzin.

We were back at the restaurant Karzin had brought me to the other night. As much as I didn't regret dragging him out of the restaurant to make love in our new home, I did regret not getting a chance to eat here.

"Try to behave," he winked.

"Can you two please not flirt? I'm trying to enjoy free bread," Cassie groaned from across the table.

"Don't eat too much," my mother chided. "Our new food storage unit won't be installed until tomorrow. If you don't finish your dinner, we can't take leftovers."

"I'm not worried about finishing my dinner," Cassie replied with a laugh. I couldn't remember the last time I heard her genuinely laugh.

"Have you got your appetite back now that you're not working at Orlin's anymore?" Helix asked.

"What happened? He's been singing your praises to me since you started," I said.

"The deep fryer freaked me out," Cassie shrugged. "Besides, I decided to volunteer at a refugee shelter. A lot of people need help."

My mouth fell open in surprise.

"That's amazing, Cass. I'm very proud of you." I reached over to give her a shoulder squeeze. She shrugged me off and rolled her eyes, but I could see her hidden smile.

"Annie tells me you're working at a shipping office, is that right, Helix?" Karzin asked.

"Yes," my brother nodded. "Lots of resources need to be spread around. I look at what's needed where and direct accordingly."

"Impressive," Karzin nodded.

Now that I was on General Rouhr's payroll, I was able to give more to my family.

It was amazing, but maybe not a surprise, what a difference it had made as soon as they moved into the new house. When you didn't have to worry about day-to-day issues like finding enough to eat, or have to live almost piled on top of each other, tempers eased.

Jokes were funnier.

Our family would never be the same as before the war, but it was much closer to how we'd been.

Normal.

Happy.

My mother now worked as a bookkeeper in a new shop that had opened a few blocks from my office. My father still spent most of his time going town to town offering his help for free, but between me, Karzin, Helix, and my mother, their finances were finally stable again.

Color had returned to all of their cheeks. Helix looked less haunted. Cassie looked less surly. The worry line between my mother's brows had nearly disappeared completely.

It wasn't just my life that was greatly improved since I met Karzin.

I still ate like we were going to run out of food at any minute, as did the rest of my family. It was going to take a while to break that habit.

When our server came back to check on us, he was shocked to see that we'd cleaned our plates.

"I take it the food was good?" he laughed as he cleared out plates. "I'll have dessert out in just a moment."

"I don't remember ordering dessert," I frowned.

"I ordered in advanced," Karzin said. "We're celebrating tonight."

"We are?" I asked. "What?"

"That depends," Karzin chuckled and stood.

"What are you doing?" I felt silly asking so many questions but Karzin was acting strangely.

I looked at my family, they all were grinning from ear to ear, even Cassie. "What's wrong with all of you? You're creeping me out." I looked back to Karzin.

He knelt on one knee in front of me and reached into his pocket.

"What are you doing?" I asked again.

"Andromeda Parker, you've made me feel whole again. I want to spend the rest of my days by your side." Karzin pulled a little black box out of his pocket and opened it to reveal a pale green gem on a black band. "Will you marry me?"

Tears were already streaming down my face.

"Yes!" I sobbed. Karzin pulled me in for a gentle kiss before slipping the ring on my finger. My family cheered and clapped for us. Right on cue, our server brought out a beautifully decorated cake.

"How long have you been planning this?" I asked once I regained a fraction of my composure. I clung to Karzin as if sitting beside each other would put too much space between us. Karzin laughed and rubbed my back through the fabric of my dress.

"A few weeks," he admitted.

I looked at my family. My mother was crying and everyone was smiling.

"All of you knew, didn't you?" I gasped.

"Who do you think told him how to propose like a human?" Helix laughed.

"We tried to tell him to buy a diamond, but he thought they were too boring," Cassie laughed.

"I still think they're too boring," Karzin replied. "That's why I made this one instead."

"You made this?" I gasped, and looked back down at the ring on my finger.

"Is that not the standard human practice?" he asked.

"Usually people buy rings that are already made," I explained. "But this is so much better."

"I'm glad you like it," Karzin grinned.

"Like it?" I laughed. "I love it!"

"Did I do the proposing part correctly?"

"You did it perfectly." I took his hand in mind and gave it a squeeze.

"Good, because it's not over yet."

"What?" I blurted.

"I've proposed to you like a human. I still need to propose to you as a Valorni," he explained.

A shiver of excitement ran down my spine.

"What does that entail?" I asked, half-hoping this wouldn't be anything too shocking for my family.

"First, I have to present a trophy to you. Usually, it's

the body of a massive beast I hunted down, but I figured you wouldn't like that very much," he laughed. "So, we're going to call this cake the trophy."

"Good call." I was starting to cry again. My beautiful ring sparkling in the light as I wiped away my tears. "What happens after that?"

"Then I make my declaration. If you like it, you accept it, and then we feast on the trophy."

"By all mean, declare away!" I laughed. This was all too good to be true. Karzin nodded his head in a playful bow.

"Beautiful creature," he began, "I offer this bounty to you, to show you that there is no beast strong enough to keep us apart. You are the brightest star in the galaxy. Allow me the honor of guarding you. I only ask that you allow me to bathe in your light. Will you accept my offer and be my lifemate?"

"Absolutely," I sighed.

Karzin leaned in for another kiss. When he tried to pull away, I brought his lips right back to mine. I'd never, ever get enough of this man.

"Now we shall enjoy the fruits of my hunt," he gestured grandly to the cake.

"I think I liked that better than the human proposal," I sniffled, dabbing at my eyes once again.

"Me, too," Karzin laughed.

"Do I still call you my son-in-law?" my father asked Karzin.

"I don't know what that means," Karzin tilted his head to one side, "but if you want to call me that, I'd be honored."

"Excellent," my father cheered. "It's about time one of my children settled down."

"Thanks, Dad." Cassie rolled her eyes.

"Your mother won't get off my back about wanting grandbabies," my father replied. "So, if I have to harass you kids over it to make her stop, I'll do it."

"Care for an offering?" Karzin asked, holding a fork full of cake up to my mouth.

I took a bite. It was delicious. I never thought I'd get to experience food like that again.

"That's way better than some dead space beast," I joked.

"I'm starting to think all Valorni should do their offerings this way," Karzin agreed.

"Annie, love! Let's talk about the dress you're going to wear," my mother gushed.

"And so it begins," I laugh.

"What dress is she talking about?" Karzin asked.

I gave my family a puzzled look. "Did you only tell him about the proposal, but not the wedding?"

"That's all he asked about," Helix replied.

"I don't know about the wedding part," Karzin replied. My entire family started laughing.

"Buckle up, Karzin." My brother clapped Karzin on the shoulder. "You're in for a hell of a ride."

Karzin looked to me. "Should I be concerned?"

"Absolutely," I nodded. "But for now, let's just enjoy dessert."

"That doesn't make me feel any less concerned," Karzin chuckled. "Whatever this wedding is, I'm up for it. I love you too much to turn back now."

"I love you, too," I grinned as I fed him a piece of cake.

We stayed at the restaurant for a long time after we ate the last bite of cake. My mother had planned half my wedding by the time we left.

We shared a round of hugs as we said goodbye to each other in front of the dark restaurant.

Even Karzin got a hug from my mother and sister.

We watched my family walk away before lacing our fingers together and strolling to our home, enjoying a sky full of stars and the promise of a happy future.

LETTER FROM ELIN

Hey! *waves*

I'M SO TICKLED to be back to Conquered World. We'll have a whole new enemy to fight, cities to rebuild, and lots of fun with our new couples.

Next up? Rokul. And honestly, nothing really sums the book up better than this little bit of conversation:

> *"It's lucky for you I was out here," he said. "If I hadn't been looking for a botanist, I wouldn't have heard you scream."*
>
> *"A botanist?" I blinked.*
>
> *"Yeah, they're like gardeners, but with more science. Did you see anyone else out here before you were grabbed by that thing?"*

Handsome, yet dense.

Terrible combination.

"I'm the botanist. Why are you looking for me?" I demanded.

"You're Dr. Briar?" Now he was the one who looked surprised. "You're not a man?"

"Last time I checked, I wasn't," I replied, glancing down at my chest. Yup. Still there.

To his credit, he got past the woman thing pretty quickly.

"You remember your friend Leena? The one you blew off today in favor of tangling with a death plant?" he asked.

"I didn't mean to blow her off," I said quickly. "Did she send you to fetch me?"

"My general did," the Skotan said. "I'm not allowed back on duty until I bring you to the capital."

"Wow. Did you piss him off or something?" I folded my arms across my chest.

His face fell a bit. "Yes, I did."

Handsome and dense, but also honest. Less of a terrible combination.

Slightly.

Keep reading for a sneak peek!

XOXO,

Elin

ROKUL: SNEAK PEEK

Tella

I've never believed in expectations.

The way I see it, expectations only guarantee the promise of disappointment.

I approached Rigkon with absolutely zero expectations, yet somehow still managed to be disappointed.

Rigkon was a new town. A bunch of them were springing up all over Ankou as more displaced refugees needed homes. The Xathi had done more damage than I initially realized. Rigkon was near where Fraga used to be.

There were plans in the works to rebuild Fraga, but it wasn't a priority at the moment. The capital city,

Nyheim, was still in the process of rebuilding. Progress was moving quickly, but it was a big city.

Small, currently useless cities, like Fraga, would have to wait.

Rigkon had an identity crisis. It wanted to be an outpost for construction crews when the time came to start rebuilding Fraga. It also wanted to be part of Fraga when the time came.

There was a handful of squat bungalows where the twenty or so permanent residents lived, a sad market with three half-empty stalls, and a long squat building that looked suspiciously like a bar.

I didn't get my hopes up. I couldn't live with the disappointment if it turned out to be something else.

If I hadn't decided to cram this gig in before starting my lab job, I'd never have known this place was here.

Before the Xathi invasion, this area was nothing but thick forest occasionally punctuated by a picturesque clearing that could've been lovely for picnics if it weren't for the aggressive flora. The Xathi had ravaged the landscape as they tore from human settlement to human settlement.

Rigkon's developers barely had to clear out any trees to make the faint dirt trail that served as the only road, not that anyone here had need of a road. I guessed it was an attempt to make the little outpost look more official.

For all of its faults, Rigkon had one thing going for it.

It was a botanist's heaven.

That's what had brought me here in the first place. I saw an ad for a small job and took it on a whim. I needed the extra cash.

I still didn't have quite enough for my own place, even though I was due to start a stable job soon. It would be my first one since before the Xathi invasion. Since I'd be in the area, I'd promised an old contact a consult on a different project once I got to town.

But that wasn't until...

Wait, shit.

I checked the date reader strapped around my wrist. It was frozen, like it had been for two days. Rigkon didn't have any transmission signal.

It wasn't part of the shuttle system, either. I wish I'd known that before taking the job. I'd been walking along old roads and hitching rides for a day and a half now.

I was supposed to start my new job at the lab today.

Before I came out here, I sent a message to the lab where I'd recently been hired. I mentioned that I'd be coming out to Rigkon on a one-time gig, but should be back in time to start on the agreed date. Now I had no chance of getting a message through out here. And I hadn't thought to message my contact about the other project.

I couldn't resist this gig. It was one of the few opportunities offering fieldwork. I lived for fieldwork.

I wasn't meant to be cooped up in a lab squinting into vials, monitors, and datasheets. It was a pity fieldwork didn't pay as well as lab jobs.

I would at least be gathering hazard pay.

I pulled out my datapad and checked the info I'd been sent when I accepted the job in Rigkon. It didn't say much other than I was supposed to meet a man called Gille in a place called Crooked Swiggen.

I squinted against the sunlight, looking for anything that bore such an odd name. Sure enough, that squat little building had a faded C above the doorway. Since I didn't see anything else that could be the Crooked Swiggen, I made my way over.

The door didn't fill the doorway. There was about a foot of space between the top of the doorway and the top of the door. There was a similar gap at the base of the door, as well. There wasn't a doorknob or a handle. I bumped the door with my knee, letting it swing into the darkened interior of the Crooked Swiggen.

I'd never seen a sorrier-looking bar.

A slab of wood lined with mismatched barstools took up the wall to my left. Whoever owned this place had built shelves big enough to hold an impressive amount of spirits, however, there were less than ten bottles on display. Over half of them were empty.

A few mismatched chairs and tables dotted the dirty floor. Only one table was occupied. Two men with skin as dark and wrinkled as tree bark hunched over matching mugs of something or other. They didn't look up when I entered, leaving me to assume that the lone man sitting at the bar was Gille.

His pants were so dusty, I couldn't tell what color they had once been. His work boots were splattered with thick mud. He'd obviously been out in the forest recently. Gille's skin was dark from many hours spent under the sun. His chin was covered with dark stubble speckled with flecks of silver.

Gille had a disappointing face. Nothing remarkable whatsoever. If I saw him in a crowd, I wouldn't be able to pick him out.

"Are you lost?" he asked blandly when I approached.

"Unfortunately, I'm not." I placed my bag on the bar and hopped up onto one of the stools. It felt like it was going to fall apart under my weight. "You Gille?"

"Yeah." He looked confused, yet still managed to give me a once over.

I rolled my eyes. I wanted to order a drink, but Gille likely wanted me to start working right away. I didn't want to have anything in my system when I went out in the forest.

"I'm Tella Briar, your botanist," I clarified.

Gille had the audacity to scoff.

I glared at him. "What?"

"I wasn't expecting a woman, that's all. Not a lot of female botanists work outside of labs these days." At least he was honest.

"Yeah, I'm a real treasure," I quipped. "Tell me more about the job. Your ad was pretty sparse."

"I didn't want to scare off prospective takers," Gilles replied. He took a long swig of whatever foul-smelling drink he had.

"That's not a good sign." I couldn't help but feel excited. This was exactly what I was looking for. "Tell me the details."

"We've had some unusual encounters with kodanos," Gilles explained. "They've been making life hard for us. One destroyed a food shipment last week. We had to live off potatoes and beet stew until the next one came. There's a particular kodanos out there that's terrorizing unarmed shipments."

"That doesn't seem very unusual," I frowned.

"It's hard to explain. They seem angry or something, but this one kodanos has just gone crazy. This guy is terrorizing anything and everything that moves." Gille muttered into the bar. "Anyway, it doesn't matter. I'm not giving you the job. It's too dangerous for a little thing like you to go up against it."

Without thinking about it, I reached for the hilt of my hunting knife and gripped it hard. I wasn't going to stab him or anything, but I wouldn't mind him knowing I could.

"Have you had many replies for your ad?" I asked. Gille didn't answer, which was answer enough for me.

"Okay," I shrugged. "Hope you like potato and beet stew."

"Wait," Gille said quickly. "If you really think you can handle that kodanos, I'll hire you. If you get hurt, it's not my problem."

"Pay me half now and half when I get back." I took my datapad out of my bag and dropped it in front of him. He looked at me to see if I was joking. I lifted one brow.

"Fine." He transferred half of the payment into my account and slid the datapad back to me.

"Thanks." I smiled brightly and tucked the datapad away. "Any place where I can get some supplies?"

"Market's in the lot next to this place. There's a store on the other side of the market." Gille spoke without looking at me. I knew I'd been dismissed. I left the bar feeling excited. I didn't know Rigkon had a shop.

This would be easy money. Kodanos were a walk in the park for me. I'd handled dozens, maybe even hundreds.

The supply store was just as grimy and dark as the Crooked Swiggen. Bunches of dried plants hung from the ceiling. Chipped and broken knickknacks lined the crooked shelves. I didn't see a shopkeeper.

I moved farther into the store, looking for anything that might be useful.

A dented canteen caught my eye. I'd lost mine moving around after the invasion, so I snagged it. I could probably fill it at the Crooked Swiggen. After another loop around the shop, I didn't find anything besides the canteen. Still, there was no shopkeeper to be seen. I stepped up to the register, thinking there might be a bell or something. There wasn't.

"Hello?" I called out, though I knew I wouldn't get an answer. There wasn't a backroom in this shop. After waiting a few more minutes, I left the shop with the canteen in hand.

The three stalls at the market were occupied. I walked up to the first one, manned by a large woman with a wide, friendly face.

"Excuse me, do you know who runs the shop?" I asked. "I want to buy this."

"Oh, I run it, dear!" she said brightly. "I saw you go in. I figured you'd come looking for me. I have a good sense about people."

"Right." I wasn't sure what to say. "How much?"

The woman's smile never faded as she rung me up. I

wondered if she consciously forced herself to keep her smile on or if she genuinely was that happy.

"Thanks." I nodded and walked away.

As I passed the last stall, something caught my eye. Amidst the sparse piece of useless junk was a silver dart. The base of the dart was filled with deep red liquid.

"What's this?" I asked.

"Toxins from the glands of Narrisiri," the stall keeper said. My eyes lit up.

"I'll take it!" I didn't care how much it cost.

Narrisiri toxin was hard to come by. I tucked the dart into a safe place in my utility bag. After stopping back into the Crooked Swiggen for some water, I marched into the thick forest, eager to be in my element once again.

Rokul

"General Rouhr just called us in for a meeting."

I looked up. It was my brother, Takar. He had a habit of walking into my room without knocking.

If it was anyone else, it would've angered me, but Takar and I had shared a room for most of our lives. In fact, this was the first time we'd had separate rooms.

We lived in a run-down building on the outskirts of Nyheim. It was one of the few buildings in the capital city that still had its original walls. The Xathi just barely missed this one, which wasn't actually a good thing. The landlady, a tiny human woman named Hellin, was nearly one hundred years of age would be buried up to her frail neck in repair bills making it safe again.

In addition to paying our rent, Takar and I fixed whatever we could for her so she wouldn't have to hire someone. It seemed like the least we could do. Most of the humans on Ankou weren't afraid of us anymore, but that didn't mean they were opening their homes for us to permanently reside.

When Hellin first saw us, two tall Skotan brothers loaded with weapons, she didn't even flinch. That's how we knew this would work out.

By now, Hellin doted on us as if we were kin.

I didn't mind humans, I thought they were fragile, and maybe a little stupid, but not Hellin. I'd kill for Hellin if she said the word.

"What about?" I asked.

"What do you think?" Takar gave me the look he's been giving me since we were children and he realized he was the smart one.

"Giant killer plant?" Takar nodded.

Yes.

I bet General Rouhr was finally ready to authorize an attack on the gigantic sentient plant we'd apparently awakened during our final battle with the Xathi.

I didn't fully understand what it was, none of us did. My strike team leader, Karzin, was one of the first people to see it, though he didn't get a good look. All we knew was that it was incalculably large, secreted a memory-altering gas, and was capable of attacking human settlements without warning from under the ground.

When it first began its attacks, there were sometimes as many as three a day. There were human casualties, but not nearly as many as there had been when the Xathi invaded. Less than thirty humans had lost their lives in these attacks.

Now, the attacks seemed to have slowed.

No one knew why.

And that wasn't comforting at all.

"When's the meeting?" I asked.

"Right now." Takar was ready to go. He made a show of looking impatient while I scrambled to get my gear together.

He might be smarter, he might be more organized and logical, but I was the better warrior. There was no contest.

Takar even admitted it once, though he said it was only because I acted before I considered consequences.

I wouldn't say he was wrong.

Our lodging was a ten-minute walk from General Rouhr's fancy new office. Our operation had two floors to itself, as well as a lab. I wasn't sure what was on the other floors. I didn't care, honestly.

We were the last ones to arrive. General Rouhr looked annoyed.

"Now that the rest of my team is here," Karzin gave Takar and me a pointed look, "are we ready to begin?"

"Dr. Dewitt, has your associate arrived?" General Rouhr asked the petite blonde doctor who even I'd be hesitant to go against in a fight.

Leena's sharp mouth grew tight.

"No," she said, clearly irked. "Apparently, Dr. Briar left a message nearly two days ago telling the laboratory about doing a quick job in Rigkon, and she must've gotten sidetracked."

"What is she talking about?" I whispered to Karzin.

"Weren't you listening at the last meeting?" Karzin lifted his brows.

"I must've forgotten," I grinned. Karzin rolled his eyes.

"Leena has a colleague who's supposedly some kind of botanical expert. The general thinks the botanist can help us understand what we're up against," Karzin explained.

"Why are we bringing in some botanist?" I asked.

"Do you have an objection, Rokul?" General Rouhr said.

"Uh." I stood up straight. "No, sir. I was simply

curious. If we're looking for information about this plant-thing, wouldn't Jeneva be the appropriate candidate for such a job?"

"Jeneva's a naturalist," Leena cut in. "She can tell us everything under the sun about known plant species, but she can't tell us much about new ones. And brilliant as she is, she doesn't have much official laboratory training that could also assist us with this puzzle."

"Exactly," General Rouhr nodded, but I could tell there was more to it. There was a hint of worry in his eyes.

"Is that all, sir?" I asked, though it wasn't my place. Then again, I was never one for staying in my place.

"Since you're all bound to find out anyway, I might as well tell you now." General Rouhr nodded solemnly. "Jeneva is experiencing some complications with her pregnancy."

Concerned murmurs spread throughout the room and I felt guilty for bringing it up. All of us were fond of Jeneva. She was plucky. I liked that in a friend. I suddenly felt bad for not talking to her as much as I should've.

"Will she be okay?" Karzin asked.

"Yes," General Rouhr nodded. "She just needs to be on bedrest most of the day. She is, after all, the first human to carry a Skotan child. There's bound to be some complications."

That was most likely a massive understatement. Skotan babies develop their scales in the womb and the period of formation is quite uncomfortable for Skotan females. It must be even more uncomfortable for human females.

With a shudder, I put it out of my mind.

She was a tough woman. She would be fine.

I hoped.

"Did you say that botanist isn't here?" I asked Leena, who nodded curtly. "Shouldn't we explore alternate methods of dealing with that thing out in the desert?"

"Do you want to run this meeting, Rokul?" General Rouhr asked. "You certainly seem to have a lot of ideas."

"We're restless, General!" I threw my hands up. "We've known about this thing for over a week. It's killing people and destroying buildings, yet somehow, it's still alive. Why aren't we out there tearing it to shreds and protecting our planet?"

"You're out of line," General Rouhr warned me.

"I apologize, General. I simply don't see what a gardener with access to a fancy lab can do to help us solve this problem, especially when we have an arsenal at our disposal," I countered.

"Rokul," Takar muttered in warning.

"Don't scold me for wanting answers," I snapped. "Karzin, Annie is a sweet female and she's very smart. I'm impressed with the information she was able to uncover, but I don't see what more information we need. We know the thing is dangerous, we know it's toxic. Why not take it out with a well-executed aerial attack?"

"How do we kill it?" General Rouhr asked. "You seem to have thought everything through. Tell me how to kill it."

"A couple of grenades will kill just about anything," I shrugged.

"And if that doesn't work? We'll have lost some grenades and angered that thing even more," General Rouhr replied. "What are the consequences of killing such a massive creature that may be deeply entangled with the planet?"

"We won't have to deal with that thing attacking cities and wiping people's memories," I said.

"What will happen to the integrity of the land mass, removing something so large?" General Rouhr asked. "How will it affect the ecosystem? Man-made resources are in short supply thanks to the Xathi destroying a large part of Duvest's manufacturing district. The humans are relying on natural resources now more than ever. Will killing this creature affect that?"

"Why would it?" I scoffed.

"I don't know, but do you know for a fact that it won't?" General Rouhr demanded.

"I suppose not," I replied reluctantly.

"Now you know why we need more information. Killing this creature might do more harm than good. In such a turbulent time, we can't afford to make any mistakes," General Rouhr said.

"I, and the rest of the humans, appreciate the sentiment, General," Leena smiled. "However, my friend isn't here and we still have to come up with something."

"Do you know any other botanists?" General Rouhr asked.

"No, but I can ask around. Maybe some of my old colleagues from the university know someone else," Leena suggested.

"Great. Get working on that. Where did you say your friend went?"

"Rigkon. I've never heard of it," Leena shrugged.

"It's an outpost of sorts," Vidia, General Rouhr's human mate, spoke up. Since the Xathi were defeated, Vidia has been at the forefront of rebuilding human settlements.

"Of sorts?" General Rouhr repeated.

"It was meant to be the first step in rebuilding Fraga, but funds had to be redirected at the last minute." I didn't miss the hint of sadness in her voice. Vidia used to be the mayor of Fraga. I wasn't entirely sure what that meant, exactly. Skotan governments didn't have anything like it. But I knew that it was a person of importance and I knew she took the destruction of Fraga hard.

"Ah," General Rouhr said softly. "Well, in that case, since we know where it is, I'm going to send someone to retrieve this botanist."

Personally, I didn't think it was worth the trouble. Unfortunately for me, my thoughts must've been written all over my face.

"Rokul." The general's voice was too perky and his smile was too big. That never, ever boded well for anyone. "I think this is exactly the sort of job you're suited for."

"An errand job?" I tried not to scoff. I was already in enough trouble.

"Yes," General Rouhr replied. "It'll give you some time to get to know our new colleague. Perhaps the botanist can help you understand why we can't just blow up the creature out in the desert, since I'm not getting through to you."

"Yes, sir," I muttered.

Beside me, my brother and the rest of my strike team tried to hold back their laughter, and failed.

PLEASE DON'T FORGET TO LEAVE A REVIEW!

Readers rely on your opinions, and your review can help others decide on what books they read. Make sure your opinion is heard and leave a review where you purchased this book!

Don't miss a new release! You can sign up for release alerts at both Amazon and Bookbub:

bookbub.com/authors/elin-wyn

amazon.com/author/elinwyn

For a free short story, opportunities for advance review copies, release news and the occasional cat picture, please join the newsletter!

https://elinwynbooks.com/newsletter-signup/

And don't forget the Facebook group, where I post sneak peeks of chapters and covers!

https://www.facebook.com/groups/ElinWyn/

DON'T MISS THE STAR BREED!

Given: Star Breed Book One

When a renegade thief and a genetically enhanced mercenary collide, space gets a whole lot hotter!

Thief Kara Shimsi has learned three lessons well - keep her head down, her fingers light, and her tithes to the syndicate paid on time.

But now a failed heist has earned her a death sentence - a one-way ticket to the toxic Waste outside the dome. Her only chance is a deal with the syndicate's most ruthless enforcer, a wolfish mountain of genetically-modified muscle named Davien.

The thought makes her body tingle with dread-or is it heat?

Mercenary Davien has one focus: do whatever is necessary to get the credits to get off this backwater mining colony and back into space. The last thing he wants is a smart-mouthed thief - even if she does have the clue he needs to hunt down whoever attacked the floating lab he and his created brothers called home.

Caring is a liability. Desire is a commodity. And love could get you killed.

https://elinwynbooks.com/star-breed/

ABOUT THE AUTHOR

I love old movies – *To Catch a Thief, Notorious, All About Eve* — and anything with Katherine Hepburn in it. Clever, elegant people doing clever, elegant things.

I'm a hopeless romantic.

And I love science fiction and the promise of space.

So it makes perfect sense to me to try to merge all of those loves into a new science fiction world, where dashing heroes and lovely ladies have adventures, get into trouble, and find their true love in the stars!

This book is a work of fiction. Any similarity between the characters and situations within its pages and places or persons, living or dead, is unintentional and co-incidental.

www.ingramcontent.com/pod-product-compliance
Lightning Source LLC
Chambersburg PA
CBHW070738180626
46818CB00007B/2900

* 9 7 8 1 9 4 0 9 2 4 5 6 4 *